# A Prayer for Thérèse

ELIZABETH STRUTHERS

Suite 300 - 990 Fort St
Victoria, BC, V8V 3K2
Canada

www.friesenpress.com


First Edition — 2021



ISBN
978-1-5255-8109-0 (Hardcover)
978-1-5255-8110-6 (Paperback)
978-1-5255-8111-3 (eBook)

*1. FICTION, HISTORICAL, COLONIAL AMERICA & REVOLUTION*

Distributed to the trade by The Ingram Book Company

To Evelyne and Doug Struthers. I am blessed to have such wonderful parents, and I am grateful for their contribution to this manuscript, and for their encouragement and support. Thank you, mom and dad.

# *Acknowledgements*

It is with sadness that I acknowledge the late Jake MacDonald. I met him while attending writing groups that he was facilitating. He read the first draft of my novel and inspired me to move forward with the writing project.

A huge thank you to Shelley Penziwol for her hard work and dedication to ensure that the manuscript was free of errors.

I want to acknowledge the staff at the Fortress of Louisbourg National Historic Site for welcoming me as a volunteer for two weeks in the summer of 2015. I also want to thank the staff, who answered myriad research questions and responded to my emails over the past five years.

# *Prologue*

**Louisbourg, Île Royale, September 1757**

The blast of a cannon. The *boom, boom* of musket fire. Thérèse jumped and her skin prickled with fear at the thought of an attack by the British Army. When she heard the music of fifes and the *rat-tat-tat* of drums, she relaxed. Soldiers were drilling somewhere in the town.

It was a gloomy day with an overcast sky. The streets of Louisbourg were shrouded in thick fog, making it difficult to see her surroundings. A cold, damp wind blew in from the ocean and chilled her to the bone, stinging her eyes. She pulled her shawl more tightly around her shoulders and adjusted her bonnet to cover more of her face. She walked with her head bent low to avoid eye contact with passersby. It had been a long walk from her home outside the fortified town. The cobblestoned streets were slick from the mist, and she was careful to watch her footing so she wouldn't slip. When she stepped into the graveyard, mud oozed beneath her feet. She looked down at her new leather shoes and saw that they were caked in the muck. She tugged up her skirt and tucked it into her petticoat so it wouldn't get soiled too.

She approached a wooden cross. On it was carved *In memory of Nicolas Louis Laserre, 1724-1757.* Tears came to her eyes when she saw his name. André, one of her husband's hired men and dear friend, had made the marker in his honour. The fishing hook she held felt smooth and warm in the palm of her hand. She hoped that Nicolas, wherever he was, was safe and secure too. She fingered the wooden cross that hung at the base of her throat.

"*Bonjour,* Nicolas. I pray God is with you, my beloved husband."

She hung the fishing hook to rest over the edge of the cross and, with trembling hands, she tied it on with a piece of fishing line.

"I can imagine your smile when you see what I have left for you. I know how much you enjoyed being out on the sea with a fishing rod in your hand. Perhaps that is where you are now. *Nos petits fils* miss their *papa*. They ask about you, and it breaks my heart to see the sadness on their little faces." The tears slid down her cheeks, and she didn't bother to wipe them away. "It was difficult for me to tell them of your death. They are too young to understand. André made Philippe a little fishing net, and he carries it wherever he goes. Pierre holds onto the little wooden animals you carved for him and won't let anyone touch them. I do hope God plans for us all to be together as a family again. I can't believe you are dead. You promised me that you would be careful and not let anything bad happen. I keep hoping you will return to us. You will walk through the door with a big string of fish in your hand, and there will be a twinkle in your eye." She smiled through her tears. "I pray daily to God to ask him to guide me. I am afraid, dear husband, for the sake of the children. I am afraid for myself. I don't know if I can go on without you. I don't feel confident that I can manage the fishing station as well as you did. But I know I must, if not for myself, then for the sake of the children. I must go on. We will survive."

# *Chapter One*

**Louisbourg, Île Royale, September 1757**

A loud knock on the door. Thérèse was stooped over the fire, stirring the rabbit stew. She jumped up from the cooking hearth and hastened to the door.

Who would be calling on her and the children at this hour? Most people would be eating their evening meal at this time of day. She brushed ashes from the front of her apron and tucked a loose tendril of hair back under her bonnet.

A thick fog was rolling in off the ocean, bringing with it a cold, damp mist. A gust of wind blew in, swishing the hems of her skirts. A man stood on the other side of the threshold. He stepped closer. She could smell liquor on his breath. He was a soldier from the garrison at the nearby fortified town of Louisbourg. He was one of the Compagnies franches de la Marine. His coat was beige with blue turned-back cuffs, a brass buckle at its waist and brass buttons climbing up his chest.

Something about him looked familiar. She had seen him in the past, but she couldn't remember where or when. Was it his face? His steely grey eyes? The scar on his left cheek?

Her heart thumped like a war drum.

"What news do you bring?" she blurted. She couldn't bear the thought of war. War meant more death.

"*Bonjour* Madame Laserre. I am Soldat Jacques Bouchet. I was visiting with your hired fishermen at the tavern of Georges Desroches, and they told me the sad news of your husband's death."

She caressed the wooden cross that hung around her neck.

What was the soldier doing at her door? She wouldn't invite him in.

"*Maman*!"

She turned around.

"Philippe won't let me play with his marbles," Pierre cried.

"Philippe, please share your marbles with your brother."

"Oh, *maman*, do I have to? I won't have enough for my game."

"*Oui*, you must share with Pierre." She gave Philippe a stern look.

She turned back to the visitor. He had entered the cottage. She was frightened. How would she get rid of him? What if he harmed her and the children?

"I bring you a gift to brighten your day on this sorrowful occasion," he said in his husky voice. He gave her a big smile.

She took the vase of flowers he handed her, keeping her head lowered so he wouldn't see the tears in her eyes, tears that threatened many times a day. It was a week since Nicolas died. Vivid memories crowded her mind of three of her husband's hired fishermen arriving at her door to give her and her two little boys the sad news. She could still hear the echo in her head, "*Non*, please *non*, not Nicolas," she wailed. The news had been a terrible shock, but she was somehow able to look after the house and care for the children. She did not want to think about how her husband had succumbed, and she clung to the belief that she would see him again one day. She quickly pushed those thoughts aside.

"*Merci beaucoup*. It was very kind of you to think of me today." Her voice sounded flat. She couldn't get up enough energy to show much enthusiasm.

She dared not look directly at the visitor, so she examined the flowers. Pretty yellow goldenrods that he must have picked that day. How could he afford such an expensive vase? She had heard that soldiers' salaries were barely enough to live on.

"I am glad you are not coming with news of war," she said, still cradling the vase of flowers in her arms.

"I have no news of war today."

"I see that British warships are no longer blockading the harbour." All summer, their white sails had billowed in the wind, a cruel reminder to the colonists that no French ships would arrive with essential supplies.

"*Oui*, Madame Laserre, there were rumours of a full-scale attack against Louisbourg. But last week's storm damaged many of the ships, and they were forced to abandon their mission."

Whatever relief she felt was dashed with the soldier's next words.

"There will be a reprieve for the winter months, but I have heard that several British ships will dock in the Halifax harbour over the winter so they can get an early start to their mission in the spring."

"Perhaps ships from France can get into the harbour now. We so desperately need food supplies for the winter."

"Perhaps, Madame Laserre, there will be some ships arriving later this fall, if the storms hold off."

Two little boys appeared from behind their mother's long skirts, curious about the strange man who had come bearing a gift.

"Soldat Bouchet, this is Pierre, and this is Philippe." She reached out her arm for the children to come closer to her. "Boys, say hello to our visitor."

"*Bonjour*," the children said in unison.

"*Bonjour, garçons*."

Soldat Bouchet looked around the room.

"I see you have a lobster trap over there in the corner. Did your husband catch many lobsters this summer?"

"*Oui*, he caught many. He was an avid fisherman, and he loved to be out on the sea."

He stopped briefly at a table that held some items belonging to Nicolas—a deck of playing cards, several fishing hooks, and a hang line—before going over to look at the lobster trap.

She trembled all over. Why had she let herself get distracted? If she had ignored the children's squabble, he would have not entered the cottage.

"When did your husband start his fishing business?"

"Nicolas started his fishing business the year the colonists returned from France to re-establish the colony."

"*Ah oui*, that was also the year I arrived with my company."

"I too, came that year." She decided not to give him any further information about her reason for leaving France.

"How long did the colonists stay in France after the colony fell to the English?"

Is he ever going to leave, she wondered? "They were in France for four years."

"How about giving a poor soldier a shot of your husband's best? And I hope it is not some of that foul-tasting spruce beer," he chuckled.

"It was kind of you to bring the flowers, but I am not up to having visitors today. I must ask you to leave." She could feel her heart thudding in her chest. What if he didn't leave? She walked to the door and opened it wide.

"I'm so sorry for your loss, Madame Laserre. I will come again another day for a visit. I will stop by Georges Desroches's tavern for a shot of rum. *Au revoir*," he said, leaving the cottage.

She breathed a sigh of relief, pulling the wooden bar across to lock the door.

She felt tears sting her eyes. Nicolas had loved his rum. In the evenings, he sat in an armchair by the fireplace, pipe in his mouth, tankard in hand, chatting with fellow fishermen and visitors alike. He always looked forward to the summer season, when the merchant ships arrived in port from the French West Indies, and he could replenish his supply.

She placed the vase of flowers in the centre of the table, which was set for the evening meal. She had set three places, each with a pewter plate, a big spoon, a white napkin, and an earthenware mug.

Pierre and Philippe had scurried back to their play. Philippe was beginning to resemble his father, with his big smile and a twinkle in his eye. She felt another lump lodge in her throat. Yet another memory of her beloved husband. Two months ago, Philippe had his fifth birthday. She had attended an auction on the quay and bought him his first pair of knee breeches and a vest to wear over his chemise. Nicolas smiled proudly when he saw his son wearing grown up clothes for the first time. Philippe had been proud to show them off to his *papa*, marching around the room like a military drummer on parade. Pierre still wore his little boy dresses and a padded cap, tied under his chin to protect him from bumps and bruises. It would be another two years before he would become a miniature model of adults. For now, she was content to have him as her little boy. She pulled out a handkerchief from her pocket, hidden under her skirt, and wiped her eyes.

She walked back to the fireplace to stir the stew. When she lifted the lid of the pot, a savory aroma of lovage, onions, garlic and cilantro filled the room. While she stirred the bubbling contents, she thought about her husband's dear friend, Monsieur André Belliveau. He had gone to the woods that morning and had caught the rabbit in a snare. He brought it to their home, so she and her children would have fresh meat to eat. He too, had to worry about having enough food for himself and his little daughter. It was a treat to have fresh meat. Winter would soon set in, and the family's main staples would be salted cod and dried vegetables.

Monsieur Belliveau was a wonderful support to her and the children during the past week. He had been at her side throughout the funeral procession, offering words of comfort, and later that day, he came with a big load of firewood. She was grateful for his help and didn't know how she would have managed without him. He had always been a loyal friend and employee to Nicolas. His wife had died in childbirth two years ago. Now that she was a newly bereaved widow, did he see her as a potential wife? Was his kindness meant to be more than mere friendship? She hoped not. She wasn't ready for that yet.

What were Soldat Bouchet's motives? Was he being neighbourly by coming to give his condolences? Did he have an ulterior motive and think her a possible wife now that she was the owner of the fishing station? She hoped that wasn't his reason for bringing the gift. She knew there would be pressure from the church and the community to re-marry, but she couldn't bear the thought of replacing Nicolas with another husband.

Her thoughts turned to other friends and neighbours in the community, who had rallied around her and her family during the past week. She was pleased to see so many people at the funeral mass yesterday, including Madame Peré and her family, who had employed her as a servant seven years ago. Many of her neighbours had come bearing food, even though they too would have meager supplies at this time.

She stepped outside after clearing away the evening meal. The night air was cool. She shivered. She didn't mind. She just needed some privacy. A strong wind blew, and she could hear the waves crashing against the shore. The smell of fish hung in the air from the cod fishing station that belonged to her now. She was the fishing proprietress of the dry cod fishery that her husband had established eight years ago. She was now responsible for a fleet of three fishing vessels, nine hired fishermen and two shore workers. She had heard many comment over the past few days that Nicolas was a good employer to the men he hired. He had paid them a generous wage, and they had free lodging in the bunkhouse next door to her cottage. The hired men liked returning each summer from their winter homes in France to work on his fishing station. Local merchants, and those he dealt with when the merchant ships arrived in port each summer, told her how much they respected her husband and said he was an honest, but astute, businessman. She hoped she could fulfill his role and live up to his reputation.

The wind whipped at her skirts and cold, wet tears stung her face. She let them come. She had tried so hard to hold her feelings in check all day, but now that she was alone, she let herself succumb to the emotions. Sobs escaped her throat. She grieved for her dead husband. She grieved for herself. How would she manage the fishing station without him? She grieved for her children, who had lost their father.

She heard the distant sound of drums coming from the direction of the Dauphin Gate. The military drummers were playing "Aux Champs," a signal to let everyone know that the gates to the fortified town were to be closed for the night.

The children were crouched on the floor, playing a game when she entered the cottage.

"*Maman*, *papa*'s fishing hooks are missing," Philippe announced.

"How do you know they are missing?"

"I saw them on the table this afternoon with *papa*'s hand line. They are not there now."

She walked over to the table to have a look for herself. Philippe was right. They were missing.

"Perhaps one of *papa*'s fishermen borrowed them."

She only suggested that the hired fishermen borrowed them to put Philippe's mind at ease. She doubted they would take them when they had plenty of their own in their living quarters. Where could they have gone? Who had removed them from the table? Could it be possible that Soldat Bouchet had taken them? She hated to think that he had stolen the fishing hooks when he had been so kind to bring her a gift. The vase of flowers still sat on the table. Where did he get the vase? Did he earn extra money as a labourer? She had heard that many of the soldiers took extra jobs to increase their earnings. Perhaps another visitor had taken the fishing hooks.

She ushered the little boys into the bedroom to get ready for bed. They knelt on the floor beside the bed and said their prayers before climbing under the covers. She gave them both a kiss on the cheek.

"God bless you little ones and keep you safe. *Maman* loves both of you very much," she said as she tucked the blankets around them.

"*Bonne nuit, maman,*" both little boys said.

She watched over them and hummed softly until their eyes began to close with the coming of sleep.

She crept quietly back into the main room. The house was quiet after the coming and going of visitors throughout the day, conveying their condolences to her and the children. The only sound in the room was the snap and crackle of the wood as it burned in the fireplace. She was glad to have some peace and quiet. She needed time to reflect and pray. As she did every night, she took her prayer book from the armoire and sat down in her chair by the fireplace.

Two candles burned brightly in their brass candlestick holders. One night, a few weeks after they were wed, Nicolas came home, a big grin on his face, holding a package behind his back. He handed it to her, and she unwrapped it. She was pleased and surprised to discover two brass candlestick holders. She set them out in the middle of the table with candles and lit them.

"They will give our table a cheerful glow when we eat," he said with a gleam in his eye.

She opened the prayer book to her favourite prayer. The pages of the book were worn and frayed with use. It had been her mother's, and she gave it to Thérèse before she died. She drew comfort and strength from reading the prayers. She missed her mother, and the prayers drew her closer to her. She was grateful that she could read and write. She loved reading the prayer book and looked forward to receiving letters from her father and older brother back in France. She knew many people who could not read or write. She had been taught by her older brother when she was a little girl.

After saying her prayers, she snuffed out the candles and put the prayer book back in its place in the armoire. She went into the bedroom and undressed, only keeping her chemise on. She relieved herself in the chamber pot and then crawled into the bed where the two little boys were sleeping.

She drew the curtains of the four-poster bed closed and pulled the blankets up around her shoulders.

She did not feel sleepy yet, and her worries kept her awake. She was anxious about tomorrow's tasks. It would be the twenty-ninth of September, St. Michael's day, the end of the summer fishing season, when the cod were weighed and inspected by a merchant who would purchase the fish. Nicolas was well acquainted with merchants and knew how to negotiate a good price. She knew men preferred to deal with other men and may not want to do business with a woman. She did not know how to negotiate a deal, and she worried that she may be taken advantage of and receive a lower price than a man would. Monsieur Belliveau had accompanied Nicolas to conduct these affairs in the past, and she planned to ask him to assist her. Once she was paid for the summer's production, she would then pay the fishermen and shore crews their share of the catch. She had assisted Nicolas with his accounts, so she was familiar with keeping track of debts that were owed and any transactions that had occurred between Nicolas and the fishing crews. He kept a contract for every hired man and a register to keep track of their wages and supplies they purchased from him. She had helped by filing the bills and receipts that he was required to keep.

Her thoughts turned to another worry. She suspected that she was pregnant. She hadn't had her monthly flow for at least two months, her breasts felt tender, and she had been nauseated when she woke the past couple of mornings. Her pregnancies with Philippe and Pierre had gone well, but she had long and difficult births with both of them. What if she had another difficult delivery? What if she died during childbirth? Who would care for the children? Tears sprang to her eyes at the thought of her little boys losing their mother. They had already lost their father. They would have no one left to care for them. It was at times like this that she wished she had stayed in France, where the rest of her family lived. She knew that her older brother and his family would take them in.

She thought of Nicolas and how much she missed him. He would never get to hold his newborn son or daughter. He would never hear its first words or see the little one take its first steps.

She and Nicolas had a loving relationship. This was the time of day when she missed him most. She missed his tenderness when they lay in bed together, making love. She missed the gentle way he caressed her skin and the touch of his lips on hers when they lay, joined together, behind the privacy of the curtains of their four-poster bed. What she wouldn't give to have him back, to put his arms around her and hold her close. She secretly hoped that he was still alive and on his way home to her. But when she came out of her fantasy, she knew that with her faith, God would help to carry her through these trying times. She prayed to God to help her stay strong for the sake of her family's survival.

She turned onto her side and snuggled up closer to the children. The warmth from their little bodies comforted her. She closed her eyes and finally drifted off to sleep, with memories of her life with Nicolas flashing behind her closed lids.

# *Chapter Two*

## Louisbourg, Île Royale, July 1749

Dearest *Papa,*

I pray God this letter finds you and the family in perfect health. I pray, also, that you are finding solace and that with your faith in God, you will find the strength to ease your pain and sorrow over the loss of dear *maman.*

You will be relieved to read that the Peré family and I have arrived safely in Louisbourg in June. I am keeping well and have settled in nicely in my new surroundings. We made the voyage from La Rochelle to Île Royale in six and a half weeks. We had several days of rough seas, and I suffered from seasickness. Many of the other passengers also suffered, and we spent several days below decks. The Peré children were ill for much of the journey. The youngest child came down with the fever first, and we feared she would be taken from us. The older children also caught the fever, and it took all of us to tend to their needs. We thank God daily that the children all survived and are now healthy. Other families on board were not so fortunate. Each time there was a death, we stood on the deck of the ship for a short ceremony to pray for their souls. My heart ached for those who nursed loved ones, only to watch as they were lowered over the railing to be buried in the cold Atlantic waters. When the weather changed and the wind dropped, we were all relieved to be able to go up on deck to breathe in the fresh sea air.

Every passenger on board cheered when we entered the Louisbourg harbour. It was a magnificent sight to behold. Through the fog and mist, we first spotted the lighthouse with its beacon welcoming the colonists back to their old home. When we neared the fortified town, people pointed out the spires of the King's Bastion (the name given to the military base) and the hospital looming in the distance. There was much rejoicing when we were finally able to disembark from the ship. We were taken to shore in smaller boats, and we entered the town through the big arch of the Frédéric Gate. Throngs of people crowded the quay that day. Incoming French colonists and New England troops were waiting for their orders to leave Île Royale. I have been told that the town has not changed much in the last four years, while the colonists were in France. The New England inhabitants who occupied the town during that time built a few new structures but left most of the original buildings intact. There are still signs of damage from the siege when the New Englanders bombarded the town, and there is much work to be done to make houses habitable again. Capitaine Peré was fortunate that his property was unharmed. It had been occupied by an officer and his wife. The Peré family live in a snug little house that was built with vertical logs and has rubble stone fill. The main floor has a large kitchen and a parlour. My sleeping quarters are on the third floor, in a little attic room. The furnishings are sparse but adequate for my needs.

My dear friend, the other house servant, Marguerite Pineau, sends greetings from her and her husband, Gabriel. They were most kind to me throughout the voyage to the colony, and they helped me get acquainted with my new home when we arrived. Yesterday, Marguerite and I ventured outside the town to pick strawberries to make preserves. The three older Peré children came with us, and I am afraid more berries went into their mouths than into the pots.

I was most impressed with the Dauphin Gate. It is the main land entrance to the fortified town. It is a majestic sight, with its coat of arms displayed above the big doors. Soldiers stand on the left-hand side of the entrance, and officers guard the right-hand side. At night, the soldiers close the gates and pull up the drawbridge. This gives me a great sense of security.

Give my love to brother, Louis, and his family for me.

Your affectionate daughter,

Thérèse Louise Daccarette

Thérèse chopped carrots for the soup. She put down her knife when she heard footsteps approaching. Madame Peré stood in the centre of the kitchen.

"*Bonjour,* Thérèse and Marguerite."

"*Bonjour*, Madame Peré," Thérèse replied, giving her mistress a little curtsey.

"Something smells delicious. What are you cooking, Marguerite?"

Marguerite was bent over, stirring a pot that hung on a hook over the fire. She stood up to greet her mistress.

"*Bonjour*, Madame Peré. I have vegetable soup cooking for the noon meal."

"*Oui*, that is a good choice. I've come to let you both know that I am giving you permission to attend the celebration for the re-founding of Louisbourg, which will be held today. Capitaine Peré will be attending with his company of soldiers. I will also be attending, and the children will accompany me. Thérèse, you are to get the children dressed in their best outfits before you take your leave. I also want Capitaine Peré's wig powdered. Don't forget to put out my best dress for me, and make sure the folds of my bonnet are pressed perfectly," Madame Peré commanded in her sternest tone. "Marguerite, I would like you to finish preparing the meal. I also ask that you and your husband, Gabriel, make sure Thérèse gets home safely before curfew. Thérèse, I would like you to put the children to bed when you return."

"*Merci*, Madame Peré, we will enjoy the outing, and Gabriel and I look forward to being acquainted with old friends. I will make sure Thérèse gets home safely.".

"*Merci*, Madame Peré. I will have the children dressed for your inspection and have the clothes ready for you and Capitaine Peré to wear."

"*Merci*, Thérèse and Marguerite." Madame Peré turned to address the wet nurse who was sitting quietly in a corner of the kitchen, holding the Peré's youngest child to her breast.

"Charlotte, I would like you to accompany me and the children so you can attend to the baby."

"*Oui*, Madame," she said and lifted the child to her shoulder and patted her back.

"*Merci beaucoup*," Madame Peré said, as she bustled out of the kitchen.

Thérèse watched her mistress go. She had an erect posture, held her head high, and kept her hands stiffly at her sides. Thérèse felt self-conscious in her presence. Her mismatched clothes looked shabby compared to Madame Peré's coordinated outfits. When she had swooped into the kitchen, Madame Peré was wearing a long black skirt and a long white jacket with red flowers climbing up its fabric. The brown woolen skirt that Thérèse wore was singed in several places. Her red jacket had holes that couldn't be mended, and her red and blue checkered apron had black smudges on it. She couldn't afford much on her servant's wages.

Marguerite took the vegetables Thérèse handed her and added them to the pot.

"I am so pleased that Madame Peré has given us the opportunity to attend the ceremony. I would be happy if you would join us, and I will introduce you to other people in the community."

"*Oui*, I would enjoy that very much."

She was excited to have permission to attend the ceremony. The family had been in Louisbourg for over a month. There had been plenty of cleaning, unpacking and re-organizing to get the house on Rue Royale back to its former condition. The Peré family were relieved to find that the home they had deserted four years ago had been well kept. Madame Peré had spoken many times of how sad she had been when she and her family were forced to abandon their home when the town had fallen to the New Englanders and the French colonists were deported to France. The Peré family and the other colonists stayed in France until the French were granted permission to re-establish the colony of Île Royale. Many of Louisbourg's former residents were not so fortunate. Buildings had been destroyed or badly damaged when the New Englanders besieged the town for seven weeks. During the four years the English had occupied the fortified town, they had not repaired many of the buildings, so they remained uninhabitable. She had overheard Capitaine Peré telling his wife that neighbouring homes on either side of theirs were not fit to live in. The Dugas home had been first used as the British governor's quarters and then turned into a storehouse. The Carrerot home, on the other side of the Peré property, had been hit twice by mortar bombs.

Thérèse was rarely allowed out for a special occasion. It was usually her job to stay home at these times to help Marguerite prepare the meal and have it ready when the family returned.

She was thankful for Marguerite's friendship. She had experienced pangs of homesickness during the voyage and appreciated her friend's companionship since they left France.

Marguerite had been a servant for the Peré household when the family lived in Louisbourg before the siege. She and her husband had lived on a property outside the walls. Their home had been burned down by the French troops to stop the New Englanders from occupying buildings near the fortifications. The couple now lived with Marguerite's sister and her family in a house on the quay. Marguerite's husband, Gabriel, was a Master Blacksmith, and when he returned to Louisbourg he replaced the artisan who had repaired the cannon that lined the fortified walls. Gossip was that the previous Master Blacksmith had stayed in the colony after it had fallen to the English and continued his trade to help them repair the badly battered town. When Louisbourg was given back to the French, his fellow colonists called him a traitor for staying to help the English. So, he packed up his wife and their fifteen children and fled to the Acadian settlements of Louisiana.

Thérèse met Marguerite in La Rochelle, France, when she was hired as a servant for the Peré family. She was fifteen years old and had found work to provide for herself and her father after her mother's death. She had nursed mother and stayed by her bedside until she took her last breath. She dearly missed her mother, but she knew she had to stay strong to support her father in his time of grief. He had become so distraught over his wife's death that he was no longer able to continue his trade as a carpenter. He wallowed in self-pity by spending his days at the tavern and when he arrived home at night, he fell into bed in a drunken stupor. He had taken great pride in his skill as an artisan. She tried to reason with him. Begged him to return to his trade. She spoke to him about the wonderful work he had done and how proud he had been of his accomplishments. The older man was inconsolable and would hear none of her talk. To make matters worse, they had no income now that he no longer worked. She realized that no amount of pleading would change his mind, so she worried and prayed. When the larder was nearly empty and there was no means for her to replenish it, it fell to her to work for their bread. She made inquiries to neighbours and acquaintances to ask if anyone needed a servant. A woman who lived on her street told her that Capitaine Peré and his wife were looking for a servant girl to help with the children and their household. The woman knew the family and took her to their home to introduce her to the couple. After introductions and a tour of the home, she was asked to report for work the next morning.

Capitaine Peré was re-posted to Île Royale when it was re-established as a French colony. He decided that his family would move back to their home in Louisbourg, and Thérèse was asked to join them. She had mixed feelings about the request. She thought it would be a great adventure to travel to a new land, but she was saddened at the thought of leaving her father. She worried about the state of his health and prayed to God to help her make the right decision. She knew that Capitaine Peré needed to know if she would be joining them and, finally, she managed to summon the nerve to broach the subject with her father. They had returned home from morning mass when she told him about Capitaine Peré's offer. Her prayers were answered by his response. He felt that if she stayed in France, she would have few opportunities as a single woman. He insisted that she accept the officer's offer of employment in the new world. She expressed her concerns about leaving him, but he re-assured her that he would be able to look after himself.

"Your older brother, Louis still lives in La Rochelle and he will look in on me from time to time. I want you to travel with the Peré family and live with them in Louisbourg."

"*Merci, papa.* You will always be in my prayers, just as *maman* continues to be in my prayers."

She continued to pray that her father would come to his senses and return to the work that had once given him such pride and joy. Louis was now working as a carpenter. and perhaps father and son would one day work together as a team.

With her father's blessing, she packed a trunk with her few belongings and, at the age of seventeen, said goodbye to her family in France to embark on a journey across the Atlantic Ocean.

On the day the colonists boarded the ship, she dressed in her grey woolen skirt and a grey fitted jacket. Given that it was a special occasion, she exchanged her coloured apron for her white one. She stood at the railing of the ship, tucked her woolen cloak tightly around her, and watched her homeland slowly disappear into the horizon. Would she ever see it or her family again? What would it be like to live in a new land? She was thrilled to be part of the family's excitement, to be venturing with them to their old home.

She watched Madame Peré walk across the ship's deck. She wore a long blue silk dress for the occasion. It was fastened in the front with blue silk ribbons, and the top part of the dress was open to reveal a pale blue stomacher with embroidered flowers. She smiled and greeted passengers before joining Capitaine Peré and their four children.

Madame Peré had told Thérèse that she was excited to be returning to Louisbourg. She was born on Île Royale and, except for the four years of exile with her family in France, had lived her entire life in the colony. It was home to her.

Capitaine Peré was less enthusiastic about returning to the colony. He found the weather to be windy and damp, especially during the long winters when there was snow on the ground. He preferred the milder climate of France, where he had been born and raised. Two nights before the family was to set sail, she heard him tell his wife that he was honoured to serve his King and country, even if it meant living in such a cold environment as Île Royale. Madame Peré later told Thérèse that he had been born in La Rochelle and came out to Île Royale as a cadet with the Compagnes franches de La Marine when he was a young boy of sixteen. He was named *enseigne en second* during his brief post at Île Saint-Jean. When he returned to Île Royale, he was commissioned lieutenant. After he and Madame Peré were married he was appointed *aide-major* with the rank of *capitaine*. In 1744, he was made *capitaine* of his own company.

Thérèse's memories were interrupted when three children burst into the kitchen. The two boys carried armloads of firewood and dropped them into the wood box. They were chattering about a public punishment they had seen on the quay. A fisherman had been caught stealing a bottle of wine and the crowd all agreed that he should be branded and whipped in the streets for the public to see. Their eyes were wide with horror at such a cruel punishment. A little girl tottered behind them, a doll in her arms.

"I was scared." She said and clutched the doll tighter.

"Sshh! You must be quiet, children, the baby is sleeping," Thérèse said. "Now let us go upstairs, and I will help the three of you dress for the ceremony this afternoon."

The boys grumbled. "Do we have to change our clothes?"

"*Oui*, your *maman* wants you to look your best. Now go and take off those dirty breeches and put on the ones I have laid out on your bed."

"*Oui*, Thérèse," the boys said and stomped up the stairs, making the baby cry.

Jean, the Peré's oldest child and the instigator of adventures around town, was seven. Paul, two years his junior, was the quiet one, following his older brother's lead. Both boys had been born in Louisbourg but did not remember their first home. The two little girls were born during the family's exile in France. Anne adored her brothers and followed them everywhere they went, even if they didn't want her company. She had just turned three when they arrived back in Louisbourg. Baby Madeleine was only seven months old.

The biggest part of Thérèse's job was to care for the children. She felt this was the best part of working for Capitaine Peré. She had spent many wonderful hours at the home of her older brother Louis, watching over her nieces and nephews. Louis's wife was expecting her fifth child, and Thérèse prayed for its safe delivery into the world.

Once the children were ready for the outing and the couple's clothes readied, she left the house with Marguerite and Gabriel. They turned off Rue Royale onto Rue Talouse and made their way up the hill, toward the military base, known in Louisbourg as the King's Bastion, where the festivities were to take place. They passed rows of military troops lined up on the *place d'armes*. The *boom* of artillery salutes and drum rolls echoed in her ears. Thérèse and her friends stopped as a group of townspeople, gathered to watch the union flag of Great Britain lowered. A great cheer went up from the crowd when the French flag was raised in its place. The group continued through the gate of the King's Bastion and passed the guardhouse where she saw Capitaine Peré standing in the doorway of the officer's quarters speaking with another officer. She thought he looked handsome in his uniform, a black tricorne hat with a gold braid and a black silk cockade that hung over his left eye. She was dazzled by the brass crescent moon-shaped medal that hung at his neck. She stopped and greeted him with a little curtsy.

The crowd crossed the drawbridge into the King's Bastion Barracks and into the passage, where they turned left into the military chapel.

Marguerite whispered in Thérèse's ear, "This chapel serves as the town's parish church."

"*Oui*, and it looks like the whole town has turned out for the occasion."

The town's elite, such as the Governor of the colony, civic officials and other prominent men and their families, stood closest to the chapel's altar. She and her friends stood with the other townspeople at the back of the church. The congregation began to sing *Te Deum*, a hymn of thanksgiving. She had heard it sung in France, and it made her feel nostalgic for her homeland. She brushed a tear off her cheek with the back of her hand and tried to concentrate on the words of the hymn.

*We praise thee, O God*
*We acknowledge thee to be the Lord*
*All the earth doth worship thee*
*The Father everlasting.*
*To thee all the angels cry aloud*
*The heavens and all the powers therein.*

A man moved through the crowd to stand beside her and her friends while singing

along with the rest of the people. Who was this man with the lovely singing voice? Why had he come to stand beside her? When the hymn ended, the sound of musket fire reverberated through the chapel with a twenty-one-gun salute by the soldiers on the ramparts. She felt the excitement of the crowd when they left the King's Bastion Barracks. People cheered, clapped and talked excitedly to each other.

She was still wondering who the man with the lovely voice was when she saw Marguerite and Gabriel talking to him.

"It's so good to see you again," the man was saying to Marguerite and Gabriel. "It has been such a long time since we have seen each other," he said, giving Marguerite a kiss on both cheeks and Gabriel a pat on the shoulder. "Have you been keeping well, my friends?"

"*Oui,*" Marguerite said. "It is so good to be back in Louisbourg, and we are so glad to see many old friends." She turned to Thérèse. "I'd like to introduce you to our dear friend, Monsieur Nicolas Laserre. Nicolas, this is Mademoiselle Thérèse Daccarette. She is also a servant for the Peré family."

"*Bonjour* Mademoiselle Daccarette. I am very pleased to meet you," Nicolas said and gave her a big smile.

"It's a pleasure to meet you, Monsieur Laserre."

He turned to look at Gabriel who had said something to make Marguerite laugh.

Thérèse was mesmerized by Nicolas and gave him a second look. He had a twinkle in his eye, and she liked his hearty laugh. He was tall with a muscular build. He had a tanned complexion that complemented his brown eyes. He was wearing a white chemise under a grey vest. His knee breeches were black, and he wore black shoes with knee-length grey stockings. He had black hair that was pulled back, and he wore a black tricorne hat. She blushed when she caught him looking at her too.

She was invited to join her friends at the home of Marguerite's sister, Geneviève Brunet, and her family. She was pleased to accept the invitation and was eager to be included in a social gathering. It had been a long time since she had visited with anyone other than the Peré family and her fellow house servants.

Marguerite and Gabriel lived with Geneviève, who was a widow. When her husband died, she was left to run the family business, a commercial bakery. She and her family had returned to Louisbourg to re-establish the business they were forced to abandon four years ago. The bakery was part of their home, a two-story stone house on the quay. The front room was the shop, which had a stone oven and store counter. The family lived in the rooms at the back of the house and upstairs. It was a commercial bakery for the residents of the town. People also brought prepared bread or meat to be baked in the oven, for a fee.

Thérèse was content to listen to the conversations around her. She was shy, never one to be talkative in large gatherings, and preferred to stay in the background. She sat with Marguerite, Geneviève and three other women. They talked of people they knew, who died, who had married and had babies born over the past few years. She was most interested in the places where people lived after they abandoned their homes in Louisbourg. Many of the colonists returned to villages and towns in France that she had never been to or heard of, and she imagined herself visiting these places one day. She spotted Nicolas sitting with a group of men. He was deep in conversation, but every so often, she saw him glance in her direction. Occasionally, she heard his hearty laugh and his animated voice. She did not know what he was talking about, but she guessed he was entertaining the men with stories of his exile in France.

The evening passed too quickly. The sound of the military drummers, marching through the streets, beating out the tune, "*L'appel,*" reminded her that she needed to return to the Peré home to put the children to bed. She glanced in Monsieur Laserre's direction and saw that he had stood up.

"I live outside the walls and need to be out of the gate before it is locked for the night," he said to the men.

Marguerite stood too. "It is time for Gabriel and me to escort Thérèse home."

Thérèse approached Geneviève. "Thank you for your hospitality. It was kind of you to invite me."

"You are most welcome, and please come again with Marguerite and Gabriel."

"*Oui*, I'd like that very much" she said as she joined her friends, who were talking to Nicolas.

"*Bonjour* Mademoiselle Daccarette. It is getting dark, and it is dangerous for you to be out on the streets by yourself. There are sure to be drunk soldiers out tonight. Your companions and I will escort you home."

"*Merci*, Monsieur Laserre. That would be very kind of you." She was touched by his thoughtfulness.

She and Monsieur Laserre stepped out onto the cobblestone street. Marguerite and Gabriel followed behind them.

"You may call me Nicolas, forget the formalities," he said, gently putting his arm through hers.

She was thrilled with the gesture. His gentle touch on her arm and the sound of his voice made her heart skip a beat.

"Then you may call me Thérèse."

She felt her face getting flushed from the excitement and wished a breeze would come up to cool it off.

"What a lovely name. My mother's name was Thérèse. Thérèse Marie," he said quietly.

The tone of his voice sounded sad. Had his mother died? She dared not ask such a personal question. There was a brief silence between them before he picked up the conversation and answered her unspoken question.

"There was a smallpox epidemic in 1733, and both my parents died. My *papa* came down with it first, and my *maman* got it a day later. They both died on the same day. I was spared that damned, dreadful disease. Pardon my language, but it was a dreadful disease. Many people in the community died that year, and half of them were children. I had no other living relatives in the colony, so a couple whose fishing property was adjacent to my father's land took me in. At the age of ten, I was old enough to work with the fishermen. I started out as a shore worker, helping to salt and dry the cod. When Monsieur Arbonne felt I was responsible enough, I was permitted to join the fishermen. That is when I got my love for the sea. Monsieur Arbonne and his wife were too frail to make the return journey to the colony this spring, so they asked me to continue the fishing business. I am now the proprietor of the Arbonne fishing company. I came back to Louisbourg to pick up Monsieur Arbonne's trade. My property is just outside the fortifications."

Nicolas had just finished his story when they reached the Peré home. She had enjoyed their conversation and was sorry when their walk was over.

"It was nice to make your acquaintance. I hope we will meet again sometime," he said, removing his arm from hers and giving her hand a gentle squeeze.

His touch made her heart flutter and she felt her face getting hot again. "Thank you for walking me home. I had a wonderful evening."

"I'm glad that you did, and I hope there will be many more wonderful evenings to come," he said, stepping away from the door. "*Bonsoir*, Thérèse."

Thérèse entered the kitchen to find the three older children waiting for her. They were anxious to tell her about the day's events, and each child vied for her attention.

"Where is your baby sister?" she asked when she had an opportunity to get a word in.

"She is upstairs with Charlotte," Jean said. "She cried a lot today."

"Perhaps all the noise and the gun shots were too much for her little ears." She assumed that Charlotte was nursing the baby. She had not known what a wet nurse was until she had started working for the Peré family. Marguerite told her that it was vulgar for upper class ladies to nurse their own infants. She had seen her own mother breastfeed her babies. Unfortunately, her younger siblings died when they were children.

"It is time that you three children were in bed too. Come upstairs with me and I will tuck you in."

Once the children were settled in their beds, she climbed the stairs to her tiny room in the attic. She put the candle down on the little table beside her cot, removed her clothes, and folded them neatly over the room's only chair. After reading her prayer book and kneeling to say her evening prayers, she climbed into bed. The room was dark, and the only sounds drifted in from voices on the street. She thought about her day and wondered about her future. What was God's plan for her? She assumed that her role was to work for the Peré family for as long as they needed her, but could it be possible that marriage was part of the plan? Would Nicolas be the one for her? Images of his broad smile and the twinkle in his eyes floated before her. Thoughts of his hearty laugh and lovely singing voice lulled her to sleep.

# *Chapter Three*

## Louisbourg, Île Royale, August 25, 1749

Drumbeats outside her window. Thérèse woke, feeling dazed. What was that noise? Had she been dreaming about being wed to Nicolas? The *rat-tat-tat* of the drums faded into the distance, and the sound that startled her from her dream was the military drummers beating out *réveillée,* to announce that it was time for the town to wake up. She sat up, wiped the sleep from her eyes, and remembered that today was the *Fête de Saint-Louis*. It was to be a special occasion for the community and for the Peré household. Capitaine Peré and his wife were to host their first dinner party in Louisbourg since the family's return to the colony in July. The meal was to be an elaborate affair with a four-course meal and wines paired with the dishes served for each course. She had been busy for days helping Marguerite to get the house ready for the occasion and preparing for the meal. Nothing but the best would do for Madame Peré.

She dressed quickly, pulling on her petticoat over her chemise, and then her skirt and vest. She said her morning prayers before starting her daily routine. Her first task of the day was to wake three-year-old Anne and tend to baby Madeleine. Anne was awake, sitting on her bed, cradling a doll.

"*Bonjour*, Anne."

The little girl brightened when she entered the room. She put the doll down, jumped off the bed, and ran to give her a hug. She helped Anne into her clothes and then went over to the cradle, where baby Madeleine was crying for attention. She picked her up, sniffed, and decided that a diaper change was needed.

Marguerite was already at work stoking the fire when she entered the kitchen with the children. Jean and Paul sat at the table eating their breakfast of bread and cheese. Charlotte took baby Madeleine from her and settled into a chair to nurse her.

"*Bonjour* Thérèse," Marguerite said. She walked over to Anne, bent down, and gave the little girl a hug.

"Now you go and sit down at the table with your brothers, and I will get you some bread and strawberry jam. I know that is your favourite breakfast."

"*Oui*, Marguerite." Anne said and ran to the table to join her brothers.

"No running in the house, Anne."

"Sorry, Thérèse. I forgot," she said, scooting onto the bench beside Jean.

"It is a beautiful day. The sun is shining. There's no fog, no mist and no wind. It will be a good day for the *Fete de Saint-Louis* festivities," Marguerite said as she bustled about the kitchen.

When the children were settled at the table, Marguerite took her aside and whispered to her.

"Would you like to accompany Gabriel and me to the celebrations tonight?" Monsieur Laserre will be among our friends." Marguerite winked at her. "I know that you enjoy his company."

"*Oui*, I would love to accompany you and Gabriel this evening."

Madame Peré had given the servants permission to attend the night's festivities after they had completed their duties. She was bubbling over with excitement to go to the evening celebrations. There would be singing, dancing around the bonfires and, most of all, she was excited to see Nicolas. She had met him several times at Marguerite's sister's home and he had walked her home twice after Sunday mass.

Madame Peré bustled into the kitchen.

"Thérèse! Don't stand there with idle hands. Make yourself useful. There is plenty of work to do today. I want you to have the children dressed in their best outfits. The children and I will be joining the procession through the town today, as part of the festivities before we attend mass."

Madame Peré's request was stopped abruptly at the sound of gunfire. Thérèse jumped at the loud explosions. Little Anne began to cry. She abandoned her breakfast and ran to Thérèse. She wrapped her arms tightly around the little girl. Madame Peré was momentarily flustered by the intrusion, but she quickly regained composure.

"That is the 21-gun salute to announce that it is the feast day of Saint-Louis. No need to worry, daughter," she said briskly.

The little girl stared at her mother with frightened eyes while continuing to cling to Thérèse.

"Marguerite and Thérèse, carry on with your duties. You both have lots of work to do today, and there is no time to spare. Thérèse, once the children are dressed appropriately for the occasion, I want you to set up the trestle table for eight people with the porcelain dishes."

Thérèse scurried about to dress the children for the day's events. With that task out of the way, she began to lay the dinner table. The white linen tablecloth had been washed yesterday, and she spread it over the table, taking care to smooth out any creases. Madame Peré would expect the table presentation to be impeccable.

She put two ornate candlesticks in the centre of the table and placed a salt cellar between them. A fish soup was to be served for the first course of the meal, so a porcelain bowl was set at each diner's place with a fork and spoon on the right-hand side of it. She folded eight white linen napkins and she one on top of each diner's utensils. She had just put the last napkins down when she bumped a wineglass. It tipped over, rolled off the table and crashed to the floor.

Marguerite ran into the dining room. "What happened?" she asked.

Thérèse stared in horror at the shards of glass scattered on the floor.

"Madame Peré and the children will be home soon, so let's get this mess cleaned up," Marguerite said and handed her the broom.

She swept and swept until there was no evidence of a broken glass. She had just retrieved another wine glass from the cupboard when she heard the Peré family returning. She put the wine glass in its place on the table and hoped Madame Peré would not notice that one of them was missing.

"Who is invited to the dinner party?" Thérèse asked.

She and Marguerite chopped vegetables. "There will be an officer and his wife, and two prominent merchants and their wives. Madame Peré has invited the wealthiest merchants in the community. She certainly likes to keep up her social standing," Marguerite whispered as she dropped a piece of carrot into the pot.

Thérèse looked in the direction of the doorway to make sure they weren't overheard by the mistress before she said, "She certainly likes to impress people."

"*Oui*, she certainly does."

Thérèse knew that social standing was very important to Capitaine Peré and his wife.

The guests arrived promptly at seven o'clock that evening. After greeting each other and engaging in polite conversations, Capitaine Peré and his wife invited their guests to seat themselves at the table. Thérèse approached each diner with a bowl of water and a towel to wash their hands. One of the ladies found it difficult to reach behind her neck to tie her napkin, so Thérèse tied the knot for her.

"*Merci beaucoup*. That was kind of you to help me. My hands are sore. It must be the damp climate."

"*Oui*, it is my pleasure, Madame," she said as she curtsied for the guest.

Marguerite entered with a tureen of soup and set it in the centre of the table with a ladle and diners could reach out and help themselves. The second course, stuffed vegetables and roast beef ragout, was brought to the dining room and placed on the table.

"Madame Peré likes to serve dishes that show off her wealth and prestige in the community," Marguerite grumbled when they were alone again in the kitchen. Thérèse nodded. She knew that only the wealthiest of households could afford to serve roast beef.

Finally, it was time to serve the desert, crème brûlée. Thérèse's mouth watered when she carried the rich, creamy delight to the diners and hoped there would be some left for her to sample. Several guests complimented Madame Peré for a splendid desert and a delicious meal. Madame Peré smiled.

Thérèse and Marguerite had just finished cleaning up after the meal when Gabriel arrived to join them for the night's festivities. They walked up Rue Talouse and met Marguerite's sister and her family, who were also going to the celebration.

"*Bonjour*," they all greeted each other. Geneviève embraced Thérèse. "It is so good to see you. We are pleased that Marguerite has asked you to join us. Our friend, Nicolas Laserre, is coming tonight too."

Joseph, Geneviève's oldest son, said, "The bonfires have all been lit and people are starting to gather," as he beckoned everyone to follow him.

"Who lit the bonfires?" Thérèse asked.

"We saw Governor Desherbiers using his torch to light one of them, and the other fires were lit by the parish priest and the commissaire-ordinateur, Jacques Prevost," Joseph said.

The group made their way up the hill and entered the *place d'armes*. A crowd stood around the bonfire. There were many soldiers, townspeople and officials gathered in small groups, talking amiably to each other. She heard a violin amongst the mingling of voices. It was a catchy tune that made her want to dance. She turned in the direction of the music and saw that Nicolas was the joyous music maker. He stood beyond the crowd that had gathered by the bonfire. He sang, played and tapped his foot in time to the music. He saw her and waved.

"Bravo," she called out when the song ended.

Nicolas bowed for her applause.

"Who taught you to play and sing so well?" she asked him.

"My father taught me to play the violin and my mother loved to sing. We spent many evenings singing and dancing along to the violin. I've kept up my singing and playing ever since I was a boy."

Joseph brought them each a cup of wine.

"Why don't you let me play the violin now so you can drink your wine," Joseph suggested.

"*Merci*," Nicolas said and gave him the instrument.

"I didn't know Joseph could play too."

"*Oui*, Thérèse, Joseph loves his music and can't wait to borrow my violin. He will play it all night if I let him."

Nicolas smiled, took her gently by the arm and swung her into the crowd of dancers. She smiled at him, elated with the attention he gave her and let out a peal of laughter when they twirled around in time to the music.

The song ended, and Joseph returned the violin to Nicolas. He rosined up his bow and struck up a lively tune, encouraging more people to join the dancers. Joseph and Gabriel took their turns dancing with her. When Marguerite and Geneviève took their turns dancing, she had a chance to stop and catch her breath. She stood by the fire and watched others having fun. She caught a whiff of the pungent smell of rum and turned to see a soldier standing beside her. She hadn't seen him approach and jumped at the sound of his voice.

"May I have this dance with you, Madamoiselle?".

The soldier leaned close to her and the foul smell of his breath caused her to feel nauseated. She backed away to distance herself from him. He moved closer and reached for her arm. The man was tall and towered over her. There was a vicious looking scar on his left cheek, and he had steely grey eyes. She pulled away.

"*Non, merci*, I do not care to dance."

"Why ever not? I saw you dancing earlier. Just one dance with me." He reached for her arm again and she jerked it away.

"I don't care to dance with you," she said again.

"You are certainly stubborn." He sneered at her.

"Come on, just one dance with a poor soldier." He slurred his words.

"*Non*." She shook her head. "I am staying here to wait for my suitor to return."

"He won't miss you. We will only be a few minutes." He reached out and gripped her arm again.

"Let go of my arm."

He dropped it when he saw Nicolas approach them. He scowled at the soldier who fled into the darkness.

"Are you all right?" Nicolas asked.

"I'm fine." She rubbed her arm where the soldier had gripped her.

"You don't look fine. Did he hurt your arm?"

"He grabbed for me. He wanted to have a dance, but I refused, and he kept on until he saw you coming."

Marguerite and Geneviève joined them.

"Is everything all right?" Marguerite asked.

"Jacques Bouchet was bothering Thérèse. He's probably had too much rum tonight."

"I heard he spends his days off in the taverns gambling and drinking while many of the other soldiers use their spare time working to repair the fortifications or chop wood to earn extra pay," Geneviève said.

"I've heard that he cheats, too," Nicolas said.

"No harm was done," Thérèse said, to calm their fears. "I have been having a wonderful time with all of you and that is what matters. Let's forget about Jacques Bouchet and enjoy the rest of the evening."

"I could use another cup of wine," Nicolas said to the group. "I will bring a cup for each of you."

"I will come with you and help to carry them," Thérèse offered.

"That would be splendid," he said, putting her arm through his.

They came back with cups of wine and chatted amiably by the fire. While they watched flames shooting sparks up into the air, he took his hand in hers and gave it a gentle squeeze. At that moment, a burst of silver and gold lit the night sky and the world around them shimmered and sparkled. The display of fireworks made her wish that this wonderful evening would last forever. The spell was broken when she saw Marguerite and Gabriel coming to join them. She released her hand from his and hoped they hadn't been seen holding hands.

At the sound of drums, announcing that the town gates would be closing, Marguerite and Gabriel decided it was time for them to take Thérèse home. She was pleased when Nicolas offered to escort her. This would give them more time together. He linked his arm through hers, and they headed for Rue Talouse.

He cleared his throat as if he had something important to say.

"I spoke with Capitaine Peré yesterday and asked for his permission to court you. He has agreed. Thérèse, would you like to be courted by me?"

She was thrilled that he wanted to court her but felt too shy to respond.

"Oui," she finally managed to say.

"I did have to promise Capitaine Peré that I would treat you with the utmost respect. I am only allowed to visit you at the Peré home and to take you for walks on Sunday afternoons."

"I am pleased you want to court me," she said, hearing the strength in her voice return.

"I am glad. I enjoyed my evening with you, Thérèse, and I am looking forward to spending more time with you."

"Me as well. I enjoyed the music and the dancing, but I especially enjoyed your company." She gave him a big smile.

"You have a beautiful smile, Thérèse."

She felt timid again and let out a nervous giggle. No one had ever paid her such lavish compliments before.

Just before arriving at the Peré property, he stopped walking. He took her face in his hands and placed his lips on hers. The kiss felt exquisite to her senses and she felt a hot glow that made her tingle all over. They parted at the sound of approaching footsteps on the cobblestones. It was Marguerite and Gabriel, who were on their way to the house on the quay. Thérèse was horrified that they may have been seen sharing an intimate kiss. The couples said goodnight and she let herself into the house. She was relieved that no one was able to see her crimson face. It had been a full day. She was exhausted, but exhilarated. It had truly been a wonderful evening, and she was overjoyed that Nicolas wanted to court her. No one had ever asked to court her before. She climbed the stairs to her attic room where she prepared for bed. She added Nicolas to the list of loved ones she prayed for each night and when she asked God to keep him safe, she also prayed that he would be her future husband.

# *Chapter Four*

## Louisbourg, Île Royale, August – September 1749

Thérèse woke with a start. Her heart pounded and she shook uncontrollably. Had Jacques Bouchet forced her into marrying him? Was it true that he had seized her by the arm and dragged her to the altar, kicking and screaming at him to let go of her? She sighed with relief when she realized it had been a dream. She recalled the festivities of last night and the wonderful time she shared with Nicolas. She was still thinking about the night before when she entered the kitchen.

"You are looking happy this morning," Marguerite said.

"*Mais oui,* I am always happy."

"*Ah oui*, but you look happier than usual. You have a sparkle in your eyes this morning. Is there something you want to tell me?"

Thérèse reached for dishes out of the cupboard and set them on the table for the family's breakfast. She hesitated, a plate in hand, not sure if she wanted to share her news yet. How would Marguerite feel about Nicolas courting her? She didn't want to have her feelings dashed if her friend didn't think it was a good idea. Then she relented.

"On the way home last night, Nicolas asked if he could court me, and I said yes."

"That is wonderful news! Nicolas is such a nice man." Marguerite walked over and gave her a hug. "I'm so happy for you."

August slipped into September, bringing with it the cool autumn days, gusty winds and drenching rains. When Nicolas wasn't caught up in the daily routine of a fishing proprietor, he took every opportunity to visit Thérèse at the Peré home. She was always busy with her chores, but he could join in the conversation while she worked.

On one particular Sunday afternoon, a warm, sunny day in September, Madame Peré permitted Nicolas to escort her on a walk. She exchanged her everyday blue and red checkered apron for her white one, which was kept for Sundays. They strolled arm and arm and stayed close to the buildings while upper class ladies and gentlemen promenaded in the centre of the cobblestoned streets. They passed inns, taverns and boutiques. Spruce boughs were draped over signs above the doors of establishments to indicate that they served alcohol and food. Occasionally, they greeted other local fishermen, soldiers and townspeople enjoying the sunshine. They climbed to the ramparts and looked out to sea, where several ships lay anchored in the harbour. They passed soldiers at their posts, with cannons mounted at the ready for any sign of danger. Before returning to the Peré home, Nicolas led her through the beautifully manicured gardens of the town. The fragrant flowers made her feel heady with joy, a perfect ending to their stroll.

On another rare occasion when Madame Peré had given the two servants some free time, Nicolas took her to see his fishing station, a short distance from the fortifications. They walked through the Dauphin Gate, across a wooden draw bridge, and onto a path that led them to his property. She had never visited a fishing station, and her nose caught a whiff of the foul odour of fish that hung in the air. The smell made her feel queasy, and she wondered if she could ever get used to such a stench. There were two small rowboats–he told her were called shallops–and they were moored up at a wharf. A third shallop with three fishermen onboard was making its way into shore. There was a low tide and the fishermen jumped out of the boat to pull it ashore. The voices of the fishermen carried on the wind and she heard the men say that the shallop was full to the gunnels with cod. Nicolas pointed out a storage shed that he said was used to salt the fish once they were split, boned and cleaned. The shed was also used to store the fish after it had been dried. She pointed to a row of racks near the beach.

"What are those?" They looked like tables with a platform. A layer of branches and boughs covered each platform's surface, where the cod were laid out flat.

"Those are called fish flakes. The fish are spread out on them so they can dry in the sun and wind. The shore workers turn them every fifteen minutes and we leave them there for a month to get rid of the excess moisture."

"How many fishermen do you employ?"

"There are nine fishermen and three shore workers. They will be returning to their homes in France at the end of September, when the summer fishing season is done. Two of them have agreed to stay to help with the winter fishing season."

He pointed to another building on the property.

"That is the living quarters for the hired fishermen and shore workers."

"Where do you live?"

"I am staying with the hired men until my house is built. Look over there," he said, pointing to a large trench in the ground. "That will eventually have a house built on top of it. Upright logs will be set into the ground, the poles will be filled in with mortar, and we'll put a sod roof on it. I want to have it done before winter sets in. Someday, I plan to build a timber frame home in the town, but for now this will do." Taking his hand in hers they walked back toward the fortifications.

"Thank you for showing me your fishing property. Now when I think of you, I will be able to picture you there."

They had entered the town, passed the guardrooms and walked along the quay until they reached Rue Talouse.

Nicolas smiled. "It has been my pleasure, Thérèse. I wanted you to know what the life of a fisherman is like."

She pondered his comment. Why did he want her to know that for? Was he thinking of asking her to marry him? Was it part of God's plan for her to become a fisherman's wife?

# *Chapter Five*

**Louisbourg, Île Royale, October 4, 1757**

Dearest *Papa*,

I pray that you and the family are well and safe during this dreadful war.

It is with deepest sadness that I give you the news of the loss of my beloved husband. He and two of his hired fishermen went missing at sea during a violent storm in September. The two other men were seasonal fishermen and planned to return to their families in France for the winter. It was my duty, as the fishing proprietress, to inform their wives. I wrote them each a letter and it was one of the most difficult tasks I have ever done. Little Pierre and Philippe dearly miss their *papa* and often ask about him. It breaks my heart to speak of him to the children, and I keep hoping that I will wake up one morning and find that it was all a bad dream. I thank God for the loyalty and support of the fishing crew. They have all rallied around to do what is needed on the property. They are year-round residents, and their contracts state that they are to be hired for the winter fishing season.

I have many responsibilities now that Nicolas is not here to assume these tasks. The summer fishing season ended, and the cod is weighed and sold to a merchant for shipment to France on September 29th, St. Michael's day. My shore master, André Belliveau, a loyal friend of Nicolas's, helped me negotiate a good price for this summer's catch. He was able to assure the merchant that the fish were of good quality. We were pleased to get a good price for the cod, but this year's catch was smaller than usual. The fishermen could not go out on days when they thought they might be captured by an enemy ship from the British blockade. I gave the hired men their share of the catch, and I am thankful that Nicolas discussed the accounts and the men's contracts with me. I paid their wages according to the tasks they performed and the debts they accumulated while employed on the fishing station. Nicolas kept an extra supply of rum for the men to purchase, so I was able to see what each man owed and subtract it from their earnings. Unfortunately, the fishing station did not make a profit after total expenditures, and I hope the winter fishing season will help to get us through the coldest months of the year.

I speak of you and the family to my sons, and they often ask if they will ever get to meet you. It would be a joyous occasion if we are to meet again one day. For now, the children and I will keep you in our prayers.

Your loving daughter,

Thérèse

"Someone is at the door, *maman*."

"Can you go to the door and see who it is, *s'il vous plait*?"

Thérèse stirred the fish soup that bubbled in a pot, that hung on a hook over the fire. Philippe opened the door.

"*Bonjour, jeune homme*."

The little boy opened the door wide for him to enter the cottage.

What was this soldier doing at her door again, she wondered? Why hadn't she gone to the door herself? She could have thought of an excuse to not let him in. What's done is done, she sighed, wiping her hands on her apron.

"I have brought you and your little brother gifts."

Pierre appeared at his brother's side. The little boys stared wide-eyed at the tin soldiers he handed them. She and Nicolas had never purchased toys from a merchant for the children. They couldn't afford such luxuries. Their toys were home-made by their father's loving hands. She wondered how Bouchet could afford gifts for her children.

"*Bonjour*, Soldat Bouchet. It was kind of you to bring each of the boys a gift. What do you say for the gifts, boys?"

"*Merci beaucoup*, Soldat Bouchet."

"*Maman*, can we play with them now?" Philippe asked.

"Please, *maman*, can we play with them now?" Pierre begged.

She hesitated. Should she allow the boys to play with the toys? Something didn't feel right about them. Where had Bouchet gotten the toy soldiers? "You may play with the soldiers after we have our noon meal. Now, go and wash your hands before we sit down to eat." She turned to Jacques Bouchet. "What brings you out this way today?"

"I was having a drink at your neighbour's tavern, and I thought I would drop by to see if there is anything that I can do to help you?"

She could not think of any jobs that he could do for her. Besides, she did not know how useful he would be around the property.

"It was very kind of you to offer, but I cannot think of any tasks that need doing at this time."

He propped his musket against the wall removed his tricorne hat, and hung it over the back of a chair before seating himself.

He certainly makes himself at home, she thought.

"Something smells good. What's cooking in that pot?" he asked. "Is it fish soup?"

"*Oui*, it is."

"I'm thirsty. Could you pour me a drink of rum?"

She was momentarily irritated by his rudeness. Did he think her home was a tavern where he could order whatever pleased him? She would give him whatever she had in her cupboard, even if it was that foul-tasting spruce beer. Oh dear, what had she gotten herself into with the soldier in her home? She sighed and walked to the cupboard where Nicolas had kept his supply of liquor. She felt a lump rise in her throat when she saw his favourite rum. There were two bottles, one full and the other one with perhaps two shots left. Her heart melted at the memory of her husband and her momentary irritation toward the soldier's boldness dissolved with it. She wiped a tear away from her eye and decided to pour him a shot of her husband's best rum. After all, it had been thoughtful of him to bring the boys gifts. He took the mug, slurped it down and belched. The boys giggled. She turned to face the children and gave them a stern look that meant "hush."

When the soup was ready to be served, Soldat Bouchet was still seated in his chair by the door. She couldn't think of a way to ask him to leave, so she invited him to share their meal. Her husband had often invited people to eat with them, and she knew her kind hospitality would have pleased him, although he would not have tolerated the soldier's rudeness towards his wife.

"I would be glad to accept your invitation," he said as he joined the family at the table. He slurped the last of his rum and slammed the empty mug down on the table.

"Slurp," Philippe mimicked.

"Slurp," Pierre repeated and giggled. Philippe giggled too.

"Boys, that is enough. I will not tolerate that behaviour at the table." She took down another pewter bowl from the shelf above the fireplace and set it in front of Soldat Bouchet.

"Ah, the boys are just having a little bit of fun, Madame Laserre," he said as he winked at Philippe and Pierre.

Before seating themselves, she asked Soldat Bouchet to say the blessing over their meal. His face turned a deep pink as he bowed his head.

"Dear God almighty, thanks for the food placed before us. Amen."

She had never heard such a short blessing before and hadn't meant to embarrass the poor fellow. Nicolas had always asked a guest to say the blessing, so she thought it would be appropriate to ask him to say it. She crossed herself, and the two little boys and Soldat Bouchet followed her example. Once settled in their places, she portioned out the soup and gave them each a slice of bread to eat with it.

"This is the best fish soup I have ever tasted," Soldat Bouchet said as he shoveled a spoonful of it into his mouth. "All I get to eat in the barracks is salted meat and dried vegetables. Madame Laserre, you are a wonderful cook. Monsieur Laserre was lucky to have you as his wife."

"*Merci beaucoup*." She could feel her face getting hot. She had appreciated Nicolas's compliments, but she was uncomfortable to receive them from other men.

"*Maman*, you have a red face," Philippe blurted. Both little boys giggled.

"Hush boys," she scolded, passing the plate of bread to Soldat Bouchet.

"I don't want any more bread, Madame Laserre. I get enough bread to eat at the barracks. I get a big loaf every four days. By the fourth day it is as hard as a bone, so a fellow needs a fresh loaf. Would you have another helping of the soup?"

She lifted the lid of the pot.

"I have only enough left to feed the children a meal tomorrow. I won't be able to give you another helping."

"*Merci*, save it for the children."

She busied herself by clearing off the table.

"Perhaps, I could have another shot of that wonderful rum of your husband's."

She inwardly groaned, not wanting to give him another drop. She went to the cupboard and re-filled his mug.

"The bottle is empty," she told him, holding it up for him to see. She refused to tell him that she had a full bottle left.

"What a shame."

She sighed and dumped the dishes into a pan of water. She had to keep reminding herself that he might not know any better. Many of the soldiers in the Compagnies franches de la Marine were recruited off the streets of France and enlisted as marines to avoid a life of poverty.

"Where did you get that scar?" Philippe asked him.

"Philippe," she admonished. "That is not an appropriate question for a little boy to ask our guest."

"But *maman*, it is a vicious-looking scar."

"That is enough, Philippe."

"Nonsense, Madame Laserre. tTe boy would like to know, so I shall tell him."

She didn't want to know how he got the scar and didn't think it appropriate for the ears of little boys. She was about to say so when he began.

She groaned and turned to the waiting pan of dishes to be washed. The little boys sat quietly listening while he told his tale and continued to gulp down his drink.

"When I was a young soldier, back in France, a fellow soldier owned a knife. One night, after we had played a few rounds of cards, he accused me of cheating him out of his winnings. This, of course, *mes petits amis*, was not true."

She looked up to see the sly grin on his face. He took another gulp of his rum.

"The fellow was just angry for his loss and decided to take it out on me," he continued.

*I'm sure it was true*, she thought sarcastically.

"What happened?" wide-eyed, Philippe asked.

"Well, of course, I stuck up for myself. That's what you have to do, *jeunes hommes*. You have to look out for yourself in this world."

"What did you do?" Pierre asked.

"I took a round out of him like you have never seen, *garçons*. I gave him a swift kick and knocked him to the ground," Soldat Bouchet chuckled.

Philippe and Pierre giggled too.

"Go on, tell us how you got your scar."

"I ran to get away from him, but he leaped to his feet and came at me with his fists. I got to him first and punched him in the nose. Then, boys," he said as he leaned closer to them, "just when I thought I had won the fight, he waved a sharp knife in front of me. I ran from the room to get away from him, but he caught up to me. I reached out my fist to knock the knife out of his hand and he brought it down over my head and caught the side of my face. Oh, what a sight that was. There was blood everywhere."

Thérèse shivered at the thought of blood.

"Boys, you have heard enough, now go outside to play."

"Can we take our soldiers outside with us?"

"*Non*, they stay inside where they are safe."

"Ah, *maman*, do we have to go outside?"

"*Oui*, so do as you are told."

Philippe and Pierre groaned and headed out the door.

"I must take my leave," Soldat Bouchet said. "I heard the faint sound of drums when the boys opened the door. That is the signal to remind me that I have an hour before I am on guard duty."

He slapped his hat on his head and grabbed his musket.

"Thank you again for the toys," Thérèse said, following him outside.

"*Bienvenue*, Madame, I enjoyed the meal. *Au revoir*. I'll be back to check on you and to see if there is anything you need."

She watched him walk down the path toward the fortified town. He was unsteady on his feet. He had certainly drunk his fill of rum today, she thought. He must have had a few drinks before he arrived at her door. He started to sing in a boisterous voice. It was a song her husband used to sing. *Au clair de la lune*. It went:

*By the light of the moon, my friend Pierrot*
*Lend me your pen, to write a word*
*My candle is dead, I have no more fire*
*Open your door for me, for the love of God.*

Tears filled her eyes and she let them come unbidden. The wind whipped at her cold, wet tears, but she didn't care. When she had privacy, she had to let out her pent-up emotions. The words to the song faded, and with it her tears subsided. She wiped her face with her handkerchief and went indoors.

She had just finished clearing away the noon meal when she spotted the vase of flowers Soldat Bouchet had brought for her on his first visit. They had lost their pretty yellow colour and were all dried up. For goodness sakes, why hadn't she noticed they were dead? She walked over to the vase where it sat on the cupboard. She snatched up the shriveled blooms and threw them in the fireplace. She lifted the vase and was about to wash it out when she remembered that Madame Peré had a smaller one with the same pattern, painted white with flowers and leaves, the colour of cobalt blue covering its surface. When she turned it upside down, she saw a familiar symbol on its bottom. A design of a wheel with spokes coming out of it. Madame Peré's vase also had the same picture on the bottom of it. She knew that it was expensive porcelain. Her Mistress reminded her every time she dusted it to make sure she was careful not to break it. Where did the soldier find such an exquisite piece? She started to tremble and her legs felt weak, so she set the vase down for fear of dropping it. She reached up and fingered her cross. Dear God in Heaven. Was it possible that the vase was stolen? She squeezed her eyes shut to stop the tears of frustration that threatened to spill out. *Oh Nicolas, I wish you were here with me.* An image of him flashed through her mind. He had a serious look on his face, as if he wanted to ask her an important question. She was reminded of the way he looked at her on the day he asked for her hand in marriage.

# *Chapter Six*

## Louisbourg, Île Royle, October 1749

On a bright autumn day in October, Thérèse and Marguerite walked to Nicolas' fishing property. He and his hired hands were working on erecting the vertical log structure of his home. Gabriel offered to help and was busy filling the spaces between the logs with mortar. Nicolas wanted to have the sod roof on before the first snow came. The women brought a picnic to share with the men.

Nicolas left his tasks to greet the women. Gabriel joined them a few minutes later, kissing his wife on both cheeks and complaining about his dirty hands. He and Nicolas excused themselves to wash up before eating. Marguerite spread out a blanket on a flat piece of land that overlooked the rocky shore. When the men returned, they tucked into thick slices of bread and molasses. Thérèse looked out at the expansive blue ocean. A strong wind was blowing, sending rolling white waves crashing against the steep bank below them.

"What a perfect day we have for our picnic," Nicolas said. "There is no rain and there isn't a cloud in the sky. Isn't that a gorgeous view out there? I love looking at the ocean. When I go out with the fishermen and the sea is calm, I find it hard to come back to shore. I like the rocking motion of the boat and the wind on my face."

"Are you not scared of being caught in a storm?" Thérèse asked.

"Ah *non*, that's a fishermen's paradise out there."

"You are a brave man," she teased. "I would be terrified if a storm came up while I was out there."

"It is a beautiful scene out there, but I prefer to be on land too," Marguerite agreed.

Gabriel nodded in agreement, for he was a man of few words.

After chatting for a few minutes, Nicolas asked Thérèse to go for a walk with him. He said that he had something he wanted to show her. She stood up and wiped the breadcrumbs from the front of her apron. He took her hand and led her behind the unfinished cottage.

"What did you want to show me," she asked.

"This is where I intend to plant a garden next spring."

"*Oui*, it is a good spot. There is lots of space here to grow vegetables and herbs."

"I'm glad you agree." He smiled. "There is a crumb on your cheek," he said, taking his hand and brushing it away.

He bent down and brushed his lips against hers. She responded to his touch and brushed her lips against his. The pressure of their joined lips sent a tingle down her spine. He released her and she was disappointed when the kiss ended. He cleared his throat as if he had something important to say.

"Thérèse, I would like to take you as my wife. Would you marry me and come to live with me in the house I am building? It will be our home until I can afford to build you a comfortable home in the town."

She was overjoyed with his proposal of marriage. The excitement left her breathless and it took her a few seconds to respond. She was honoured to be his bride and would live anywhere with him, even if it was a shack in the woods. She did, however, have a concern, but she felt scared to voice it. What if he thought she didn't want to marry him?

"Well, what do you say to my proposal?" he prompted.

She jumped at the sound of his voice and knew she must speak.

"*Oui*, I would be honoured to be your wife, Nicolas and I would be happy to live with you anywhere, so long as we are together and healthy," she smiled up at him. "but I am only seventeen years old. I would need my father's permission for a priest to marry us and my *papa* is far away in France."

"*Oui*, Thérèse, I have thought of that too. I am pleased that you would be happy as my bride," he took both his hands in hers and gently stroked them. "I will write to your father in France and ask for his consent for us to be wed. You can write to him, too, and ask for his blessing for our marriage. We can have our letters on the next ship to France. That way, we should have your *papa*'s answer in the spring."

It would be such a long wait until spring. She would prefer to marry him this instant, but she knew that wouldn't be possible. A priest would never consent to perform the marriage ceremony without her father's blessing. She thought of another concern.

"I would need to get permission from Capitaine Peré to leave my employment."

"Do not worry yourself about that, *ma chérie*," he said, continuing to hold her hands in his. "I have talked to Capitaine Peré, and he is willing to release you as his employee when the time comes."

"When did you find the time to sneak that conversation in?"

"Ah, I find time when I want something," he said with a gleam in his eye. "Ah, I almost forgot. I have something for you."

He reached into his pocket and brought out a small package and handed it to her. She gently fingered the little bundle, before opening it. Whatever was hidden inside was wrapped in a beautifully embroidered handkerchief, edged with lace. In its centre was a pink rose with green leaves. In the bottom right hand corner was sewn, three letters in delicate stitches: TML. She stroked the fine embroidery work and wondered who had done such intricate work.

"Those are my *maman's* initials. They stand for Thérèse Marie Laserre. She embroidered the handkerchief in hopes of giving it to a daughter on her wedding day. I found it amongst her belongings after her death. She was a seamstress and took in sewing for extra income. She could sew anything from ladies' fancy ball gowns to men's breaches. Both my sisters died in infancy. If my *maman* was alive, she would be pleased to know that I am giving it to you. But go on, open it up and see what's inside," he urged.

She carefully untied the piece of string that held the bundle securely. Beneath the folded fabric, she found a wooden cross strung from a pink silk ribbon. She was speechless. She had never owned such a beautiful piece of ornamentation.

"Let me put it around your neck for you." He reached around and tied the ribbon at the back of her neck.

"My *papa* carved it for my *maman* and gave it to her when they were married. My *maman* wore it every day of her married life. I remember seeing it around her neck. I would be pleased if you would wear it. I wish you could have met her," he said wistfully.

"*Merci beaucoup*, Nicolas. It is lovely. I will always wear it, no matter what God's plan is for us. It will always remind me of you, no matter where you are."

"I am so glad you like it, *ma chérie*." He kissed her on both cheeks. "We should rejoin Marguerite and Gabriel. They will be wondering where we are."

He took her hand and they walked back to join their friends.

"Your father was a beautiful carver."

"*Oui*, he liked to work with his hands, and I remember him sitting in his favourite chair by the hearth in the evenings, whittling with pieces of wood. He was a fisherman, like his father before him, and he spent his days out on the sea. But his greatest enjoyment was working with wood. I remember him saying that he wished he could have taken up a trade as a carpenter, but he never had the opportunity."

"We were starting to wonder where you were," Marguerite said when she and Nicolas returned.

Thérèse smiled and ignored her friend's retort.

"I have asked Thérèse to marry me," Nicolas said, a big smile on his face.

"That is why you two are grinning from ear to ear," Marguerite said.

"That is wonderful news," Gabriel said.

Marguerite gave Thérèse a big hug. "I am so happy for you."

"Congratulations, *mon ami*," Gabriel said, patting Nicolas on the back.

"If God wills it, we hope to be wed next spring," Thérèse said.

"This calls for a toast," Gabriel said. He reached into the basket lying on the blanket and brought out a bottle of wine. He poured it into pewter mugs and passed them around.

"To the happy couple," Gabriel toasted as he raised his mug. "May you have a blessed marriage," Marguerite added and raised her mug.

"Here's to us," Nicolas said and he and Thérèse raised their mugs to join their friends.

October 14, 1749

Dearest *Papa*,

I pray God this letter finds you and the family in perfect health. I think of you often, and you are always in my prayers.

I am keeping well and continue to thrive in my new surroundings.

I do have some happy news to share with you, *papa*. I have met a man whose name is Nicolas Laserre. He has been most kind to me. He is a hard worker and is the proprietor of a lucrative fishing station. With permission from Capitaine Peré, Nicolas has been courting me, and I have spent many wonderful hours in his company. I believe you would like him. He enjoys a good laugh, but most importantly, he is thoughtful and shows that he cares about me. My dearest friend, Marguerite, and her husband, Gabriel, introduced him to me. They have been acquainted with him for many years. I am sure you remember that I spoke often of them with great fondness. They have been most kind to me since we have left France. They know how much I have missed my loved ones and they have been most generous to include me in their social gatherings. The most wonderful news is that Nicolas has asked for my hand in marriage, and I said that I would be honoured to join him in matrimony. You will also receive a letter from him requesting your permission to take me as his wife. I pray that with God's guidance, you will give us your blessing to be wed.

Your affectionate daughter,

She dipped her quill in the inkwell once more and signed her name. She hoped that her letter would persuade her father to allow them to marry. She fingered the little cross that now hung at the base of her neck and wondered what God had in store for her future. She prayed that it was a future with Nicolas in it.

# Chapter Seven

**Louisbourg, Île Royale, November 1757**

Thérèse stood at the window. A torrent of rain pelted against the pane, while a fire was burning brightly in the hearth, keeping the main room snug and warm. Philippe and Pierre sat at the table, playing a game of cards. The warmth of the cottage and the children's playful chatter did not cheer her. She felt miserable and her mood matched the gloomy weather outside. Her heart ached for the loss of her husband and she wished that he could magically rise out of the mist. There wasn't a day that went by that she did not think of him. It was two months since his death, but her grief was still as strong as it was the day he died.

Another matter haunted her thoughts. What was she to do about the porcelain vase? Had Soldat Bouchet purchased it, or was it someone else's treasured piece? Did the man dare to bring deception into her home? She felt outraged at the thought. What if someone accused her of stealing it? She shivered at the thought of the punishment that was handed out to thieves. She could be put on display and marched through the streets for the townspeople to witness her shame. They would decide what type of sentence should fit the crime. She had heard of thieves who had been sent to prison or shipped off to the Mediterranean gallows. But even worse than that was hanging. She was glad that she had hidden the vase in a cupboard, away from prying eyes. But she couldn't keep the vase. What if it belonged to someone else in the town? Should she speak with the priest or Capitaine Peré? What about the fishing hooks that went missing and the toy soldiers he had brought for her sons? She had let the boys play with them once, and then she had put them away for safekeeping.

The rain let up and, as it did, she saw a man coming up the path. Her heart plummeted when she saw who it was. Soldat Bouchet. She groaned. Of all the people who could call on her today, it had to be him. She had no intention of confronting him about the goods he was bringing to her home, for fear of what he might do to her and the children. She was determined not to let him in this time. He knocked at the door and she opened it a crack.

"Why are you out on such a miserable day?" she blurted.

"*Bonjour*, Madame Laserre. I was at Georges Desroches's tavern and bought a bottle of wine from him. I thought the wine would raise your spirits on such a cold, dreary day."

She smelled liquor on his breath. She gripped the door tightly. He grabbed the door handle and pushed it open wider. Her hands were sweaty, and she lost her grip. He stepped in out of the rain and reached out to hand her the bottle. She refused to take it.

She shook her head. "*Non merci*, I won't accept any more gifts from you."

"Why ever not, Madame?"

He removed his tricorne hat. Drops of water trickled from it. She grimaced at the puddles forming on the dirt-packed floor.

"You have brought enough gifts to my home. You don't need to keep lavishing my family with expensive items."

"Nonsense, I enjoy bringing them to you."

He put the bottle of wine down on the corner of the cupboard "*Bonjour*, *garçons*. What are you playing?"

"We're having a game of war," Philippe said.

"And I'm winning," Pierre announced proudly.

"That's the spirit, Pierre. You beat your big brother."

Thérèse frowned at him. She was not pleased with the message he was sending to her sons.

He walked to the fireplace where he warmed his hands over the fire.

"That sure is a cold day out there. A mug of that wine would sure warm me up."

She trembled and her heart beat fast. How was she going to get rid of him?

"I was wondering how you and the boys are managing, and so I decided I would stop for a visit."

"We are keeping well."

"Is there anything I can do for you while I am here?"

"*Non*, I can't think of a thing."

There were lots of chores she could think of that needed doing, but she had no intention of encouraging him to stay.

"So how about that mug of wine," he insisted.

She opened her mouth to protest when the door flew open and Monsieur Belliveau stormed in. A wild turkey dangled from his hand. She was relieved to see her husband's friend. Yet, she was shocked to see the fierce expression on his face. He faced Soldat Bouchet. Anger flashed in his eyes.

"What is your business with Madame Laserre?" he demanded.

"I dropped by to check on her and the children. I brought the gift of a bottle of wine. I thought it might cheer her up on this dreary day."

"Where did you get the bottle of wine?"

"I bought it from a merchant in the town. Why do you ask? Do you think I would stoop so low as to steal it?"

He had told her a different story.

The soldier's eyes flashed daggers at him. Monsieur Belliveau glared back. She stepped between the men.

"Soldat Bouchet, I think it best that you take your leave."

He didn't move, but just continued to glare at his rival.

"Please, it's best you leave now, Soldat Bouchet."

"You heard Madame Laserre. She is asking you to leave her home. I'm ordering you to leave at once."

When he didn't move, Thérèse grabbed his arm and lead him to the door. He jerked his arm from hers and turned to Monsieur Belliveau.

"I'm leaving, but just remember this: you are not my commander." He stomped out and the door slammed behind him.

"I don't like him in your home, Madame Laserre. He's trouble. Rumour has it that he is a drunk and spends his days in the taverns gambling his wages away. I've also heard he's a poor loser. He could be a danger to you and the children. I hope to never see him on your property again."

"*Oui*, Monsieur Belliveau," was all she could manage to say. She was stunned by the turn of events today.

"How did you know he was in my home?"

"I was heading up the path toward your property to bring you the wild turkey I shot this morning and I saw him at your door. I hurried to catch up with him before he bothered you, but he got in before I reached the cottage."

"Ah, I'm thankful that you came when you did. She reached for her cross. I was just going to ask him to leave when you arrived."

She didn't share her suspicions about the stolen vase or the whereabouts of the fishing hooks. She didn't want anyone to know that there may be stolen goods in her home.

"Thank you for the wild turkey. It is much appreciated. My little ones will have fresh meat to eat! It will be a change from salted cod." She gave him a gracious smile.

"You're most welcome, Madame Laserre. I will hang the meat in the shed for you."

"Give my love to Marie-Louise," she said as he went out the door.

She closed the door on the dampness outside. Her temples throbbed and she massaged her forehead to ease the pain. She was thankful to have meat to feed the children, and this thought warmed her as she turned to the fireplace to heat water for tea. She added crushed meadowsweet to the boiling liquid. She thought the hot drink would help to relieve her headache.

She decided it was time to go through her husband's belongings. She needed to sell his best clothes for extra money to help them through the winter. It was a task she had put off as long as possible, but since it was a miserable day, it was best to get the task done. While rummaging amongst Nicolas' things, she came across the chest where she stored her own possessions. Inside, underneath a pile of old dresses and blankets, was a bundle of old letters from her father in France. She untied the ribbon that held them together, sat down on the edge of the bed and began to read. Tears stung her eyes when she read them. Even though Louisbourg was her home, she still missed her loved ones back in France. Happy memories flooded back, and she smiled when she read a letter written in February 1750.

# *Chapter Eight*

**Louisbourg, Île Royale, April 1750**

The last ship of the season left the Louisbourg harbour in early November, bound for France. It carried the letters that Thérèse and Nicolas had written to her father, requesting his parental consent for his daughter to be wed to Nicolas. She was anxious to receive a reply from her father but knew it would be a long wait. No mail from the outside world would arrive until next spring.

November slipped into December, bringing with it bitterly cold temperatures that she had never before experienced. She had to bundle herself up with several layers of clothing before heading outdoors.

While the winds howled around the buildings and the snowdrifts accumulated, people spent most of their time in doors. Madame Peré kept Thérèse and Marguerite busy with the daily chores of cooking, cleaning and caring for the children. Added to these tasks were preparations for two dinner parties that Capitaine Peré and his wife hosted during the Carnival. Madame Peré held coffee parties and invited the elite of Louisbourg to her home for these occasions.

She permitted the servants to have Sunday afternoons off from their household tasks. No matter what the weather was like, Nicolas walked through the deep drifts on snowshoes to spend the afternoons with Thérèse. When she did not want to go out into the cold, her mistress permitted the couple to visit in the kitchen where they sat by the fire and sipped angelica tea, enjoying each other's company. On other occasions, when she felt like venturing outdoors, they would snowshoe to the homes of friends and neighbours. She had never used snowshoes before and found them big and clumsy on her feet. When she first tried them on, she fell twice in the snow, causing uproarious laughter from on lookers. Many an afternoon was spent singing, swapping stories and enjoying the company of others. She appreciated these opportunities to become acquainted with townspeople, and they soon became her friends. She particularly liked to visit the home where Marguerite and Gabriel shared accommodations with her sister's family. She enjoyed the friendship of the women and learned much about married life and having children. It made her wonder about her own future and whether she would have children one day.

In early April, the days got warmer and the snow melted, leaving mud and slush in its place. There was a knock at the kitchen door and Marguerite hurried to open it. Thérèse was using the mortar and pestle to crush up a cone of white sugar into fine granules. She looked up when she heard Nicolas' voice. She wondered what he was doing at the Peré home during the week. He stomped the mud off his boots before entering the kitchen.

"Come in and don't worry about your boots," Marguerite said. "The children have been dragging mud in all morning. As soon as I get it cleaned up, another child comes in with mud on his shoes. Would you like a cup of hot buttered rm?"

"I would love a hot drink, Marguerite. I'm chilled to the bone. There is a cold wind today."

"*Bonjour,* Nicolas. This is a pleasant surprise." Thérèse wiped her hands on her apron. "What brings you to the Peré home today?"

"I was in town picking up supplies and I decided to drop by for a visit."

He sat down at the kitchen table and Marguerite placed a mug in front of him.

"It is hot and it will warm your up. I put extra brown sugar in it for you," she said and smiled.

"*Merci,* Marguerite," he said and took a sip.

Four-year-old Anne rushed into the kitchen, sobbing uncontrollably. Thérèse abandoned the sugar and ran to her. Jean and Paul hurried into the house.

"Wipe your shoes off before you come in," Marguerite ordered. But it was too late. The boys created a trail of mud as they stomped through the kitchen.

"What happened to make you so upset?" Thérèse asked.

"My knee is hurt," Anne gasped through her sobs.

"How did it happen?" Marguerite asked.

"Jean and Paul were chasing me, and I slipped on the cobble stones," she wailed."

"We weren't chasing her," Jean said. "We were playing a game of tag."

"Boys, your sister is younger than you too are, and you should be looking out for her to make sure she doesn't get hurt," Thérèse scolded them.

Marguerite lifted up the little girl's skirt and petticoat to reveal a small cut on her knee.

"It hurts!"

"There, there, child, we are going to make you better," Thérèse soothed, cuddling the little girl in her arms.

"Can you get out the dried woad and make it into a poultice? We will put it on the cut to stop the bleeding. Could you also bring me some lamb's ear so I can make a bandage, *s'il vous plait*?"

Thérèse set Anne down on a chair and went to retrieve the necessary herbs. When she returned, she picked up the still-screaming little girl and set her on her lap to comfort her.

Madame Peré stormed into the kitchen.

"What is all the commotion about?" she asked as she looked at her sons. Neither boy spoke, for fear of the punishment that would follow.

Madame Peré was stern with the children and did not take any nonsense from them.

Finally, Jean spoke. "We didn't do anything to Anne. We were playing a game of tag and she tripped on the cobbles."

"It was more likely that you were chasing your sister," their mother said.

"We were not chasing her, we were playing, Paul said.

"Jean and Paul, please come with me this instant."

The boys' shoulders slumped, and they followed their mother into the parlour. She was strict with the boys and was probably planning to give them a good scolding, Thérèse thought.

Anne's sobs subsided after much doctoring and soothing. She climbed down from Thérèse's lap to attend to her doll, lying in its cradle. She told the adults that her baby had a cut on her leg, and she was going to fix it. Thérèse and Marguerite smiled. The commotion even got a smile and a chuckle from

Nicolas. Thérèse returned to her task of chopping up the sugar and when it was cleaned up, she took a seat at the table to visit with Nicolas.

He reached into his satchel and pulled out a package.

"This is for you," he said and handed it to her.

"There is a package for me? Who is it from? I do hope it is from *papa*."

"Open it and find out," he urged.

It was a cloth bundle, tied up with string. She recognized her father's handwriting and was anxious to find out what was inside. She looked at Nicolas for any clues, but he was watching her intently, so she continued to untie the string. The first item she took from the bundle was a stack of pages folded and sealed with wax. Her hands trembled when she slipped her finger under the seal to open it.

"It is a letter from my father in France."

"Go on, read it and find out what he has to say."

Her heart thumped loudly in her chest when she unfolded the pages. She was scared that her father might have decided not to allow her to marry Nicolas. She sent up a silent prayer to God that he would give his blessing over the marriage.

> February 15, 1750
>
> Dearest Daughter, Thérèse,
>
> I hope this letter finds its way to you in Louisbourg. I have prayed for you daily, daughter, since I bid you farewell before you boarded your ship for the voyage across the Atlantic Ocean.
>
> I was most pleased to receive your letter, dated October 1749. Another letter had also arrived from Monsieur Nicolas Laserre, requesting my permission to wed you. After reading his request, I prayed for God to help me make the right decision for you, and I gave the matter much thought. My wish would have been to have my daughter wed to a man of my personal acquaintance and for myself, as your father, to personally witness the matrimony. The man you spoke of in your letter sounds like a kind, honest and loyal husband

for you. Monsieur Laserre assured me in his letter that he would provide and care for you in sickness and in health, all the days of his life. He spoke of your employer, Capitaine Jean Baptiste Peré and his wife, Madame Madeleine Peré. He thinks highly of this couple and believes that you are in good hands as an employee of their household. He told me has spoken to your employers to request that he be allowed to court you. The couple knew of his acquaintance with your companions, Marguerite and Gabriel Pineau, and were willing to grant you permission to accompany him on walks and social gatherings. In his letter, he also told me of his conversation with Capitaine Peré to ask for your hand in marriage and, if the time should come to wed you, to request that he release you as his employee. He assured me that Capitaine Peré told him that he would be honoured to release you for this reason. I have prayed long and hard daughter and have given the matter of your marriage much thought. I have come to the decision that I accept Monsieur Laserre's request to take your hand in marriage, and I wish you much happiness with this man.

The other news that will give you much happiness, dearest daughter, is that I am feeling stronger and healthier each day. I have not darkened the door of the tavern for many months now, and I am happy to report that I have returned to my trade as master carpenter. Your brother, Louis, works along side me, and we have made much progress. I feel satisfied with my accomplishments over the past six months, and I am rewarded with several new houses in the town. I continue to grieve for my dear wife and your loving mother, but every day the ache in my heart lessens. I give thanks to you, my daughter, for your courage and faith in God to help me see the way back to a fulfilling life. When I watched you board the ship, bound for a life in the new world, I knew you were a strong person. I know you have the spirit and endurance to overcome any atrocities that may come your way. Your kind and thoughtful manner has helped me to move on with my life. I thank you once again, daughter, for your faith and guidance to help me see the true meaning of life.

I have enclosed a gift for you, daughter, and I know you will cherish these items. I will keep the gifts a surprise for you. However, I want you to know that these were gifts given to your mother by her *maman,* when she and I were wed. She treasured these items all of her married life, as I know you will too.

Your affectionate father,

Joseph Daccarette

"*Mais oui!*" Thérèse whooped with joy and put her arms around Nicolas. "The answer is, yes, we can be wed!"

Nicolas whooped with delight and hugged her tight.

"I received a letter from your father today too, and I was pleased to get the same answer."

Marguerite gave her a big hug. "That is wonderful news. Congratulations to both of you! I can't wait to get home tonight to tell Gabriel the good news. He will be so happy for both of you."

Little Anne, who had been playing with her doll, abandoned her play to join the excitement. She ran over to where Thérèse stood, still clutching the letter in her hand, and gave her a big hug. She squealed with delight and jumped up and down when she heard about the upcoming wedding.

"What's this I hear of marriage?" Madame Peré asked, entering the kitchen, the boys following behind her.

"Thérèse is getting married," Anne blurted out.

Nicolas gave Madame Peré a slight curtsy and proceeded to tell her about the letter's contents.

"I will speak to your husband to request his permission to relinquish Thérèse as his employee, so that she may come to live with me as my wife."

"Very well, I will tell Capitaine Peré that you will be calling on him. I wish you both well in your life together, but I also want to remind you both of your religious obligations to the church. As you are a servant in my household, Thérèse, and you have no parents in the colony to guide you, I feel it is my duty to remind you and Nicolas to go and speak to the *curé* at the Chapelle Saint-Louis. You must have a betrothal that will include the *curé* and witnesses, and the marriage banns must be read out three times at Sunday mass before your nuptials are to take place. My husband and I expect that you uphold your religious obligations. We are upstanding citizens in the community, and we hope to keep it that way."

"*Oui*, Madame Peré. We will respect your wishes. As you know, I have a strong faith and I am honoured to obey God and the church," Thérèse said.

"*Merci Beaucoup*, I will leave you to make your preparations." With that said, Madame Peré turned on her heal and went back to the parlour.

"Thérèse, did you know there is something else for you in the package from your *papa*?" Nicolas asked eagerly.

"*Ah oui*, there is indeed. I had almost forgotten about the gifts from *mon père* in my excitement."

It was not often that someone received a package, and everyone waited to find out what else was inside. She reached in once again amongst the folds of cloth to reveal an embroidered pocket. Her eyes filled with tears of longing for her mother when she saw it. She quickly recovered when she realised everyone was watching her.

"What is it?" little Anne asked curiously, her hazel eyes wide with excitement.

"It is a *poche*," she explained, tying the garment around her waist and letting it hang on her hip.

"The *poche* goes underneath my skirt, which has an opening that lines up with where it will hang, so I can put my hand in and get out what I need."

"Can you make me one of those?" Anne asked.

"*Oui*, I will make you one before I am wed," she promised the little girl.

Anne put her little arms around her waist. "Will you be leaving me?"

"*Oui*, but I won't be far away. I will be living just outside the walls, so I will be able to see you often."

"I hope so. I will miss you," Anne cried with tears streaming down her face.

"It is so beautiful. Look at the intricate stitching that has been done, Thérèse. It is exquisite," Marguerite said.

"*Oui*, it is a beautiful piece of work," Nicolas agreed.

Thérèse looked down and admired the garment for herself. It was made of coarse linen and had embroidered flowers in magenta, fuchsia, dark pink and a lighter, delicate pink. Leaves of different shades of green surrounded the beautiful blooms. The flowers were so well stitched that they looked like little jewels. While she fingered the fine stitching, she felt something else inside the pocket, so she reached in and brought out her mother's rosary beads.

"Oh," she gasped, fingering the smooth surface of the crucifix. She felt another lump rise in her throat and tears stung her eyes. She fondly remembered watching her mother pray the Holy Rosary every night, before she went to bed. Even during her illness, she continued this ritual until she was no longer able to do so. Thérèse did not own rosary beads and was touched by her father's thoughtfulness in giving them to her. She vowed to herself that she would use them faithfully.

"Were those your mother's rosary beads?" Marguerite asked.

"*Oui*." She sniffled and wiped her eyes. "They were *à ma maman,*" she said as she held the beads against her heart.

# Chapter Nine

**Louisbourg, Île Royale, June 1750**

Thérèse folded the last of the belongings that she would take with her to her new home at the fishing station. Stockings and garters were the last items to go into her trunk. Her heart was filled with joy at the thought of spending the rest of her life with Nicolas, and she could hardly believe that tomorrow, by this time of day, she would be his wife. Looking over at the bed, she spotted the wedding gifts that had been given to her by her dear friend Marguerite and other women in the community, who had become acquainted with her over the past few months. The women had made her towels, tea towels and sheets. The most beautiful piece of work was the covering that had been made to lay over the marriage bed. The covering was made of a soft cotton and was a celery green colour. She felt her face getting flushed at the thought of being under the covers with her new husband. She had listened to women whisper about what a man does with his wife in bed, but she didn't know what to believe. Some women were disgusted by the ordeal, and said it was painful. Other women found it an arousing experience. Well, she was going to find out for herself soon enough. She loved Nicolas with all her heart, but the thought of what happens in the marriage bed made her anxious.

"Thérèse, have you seen Elsie recently?" Marguerite asked, interrupting her thoughts. Her friend was out of breath from running up the stairs.

"*Non*, I haven't seen her. I have been packing for the last hour. Why do you ask? Is she missing again?"

"I sent her out to the garden two hours ago to do some planting, and when I went out to check on her, she was nowhere to be seen and had done no work at all. Madame Peré will be furious when she discovers that she has neglected her duties again."

Thérèse groaned. "Where has she disappeared to this time?"

She remembered another occasion when the young Irish girl had gone missing. She had been sent to fetch water from the well and had not returned. She and Marguerite went out to look for her and found her on the quay, flirting with two sailors from the French West Indies. Marguerite grabbed her firmly by the arm and marched her back to the Peré home to receive the scolding she deserved. The girl had a sharp tongue and was not afraid to use it.

"Let me go, you sneaky old woman." She yanked her arm from Marguerite's grasp. "You have no business spying on me."

"Then why don't you do your job. That way we wouldn't have to come and look for you."

"Oh, stop preaching, Marguerite. You sound like my mother."

"I know someone else who will be preaching like your mother. You better keep that mouth of yours shut, *Madamoiselle*, or else you might find yourself without a job in the Peré household. Madame Peré will not stand for that kind of talk in her home."

Madame Peré was waiting for the young girl and gave her a stern lashing with her tongue. Elsie was warned that if she abandoned her chores again, she would find herself out on the street without a job.

Elsie was a slender girl with curves in places that attracted the likes of wayward sailors who were looking to pick up a woman for the night. She had a head of natural curly red hair that always hung out of her bonnet. She did her chores slowly, leaving Marguerite and Thérèse to pick up the slack. Capitaine Peré and his wife had hired her in April, when they learned that Thérèse was to be wed and would be leaving their home to live with her new husband.

"Madame Peré has asked that you and I go out and look for Elsie. The boys are out playing, and the little ones are asleep. Madame Peré has just arrived home and she said she would look after the children if they wake before we return. She is furious with the young girl."

"I don't blame her for being mad. She's old enough to know better." She closed the lid of the trunk and followed Marguerite downstairs.

The older servant would have her hands full when she left, and it also occurred to Thérèse that she may need to continue her employment after her marriage if Elsie kept this behaviour up. Marguerite couldn't possibly manage the household chores and care for the children on her own.

The women left through the kitchen door and headed for the street. Passing the garden, she heard a woman humming to herself. It was Elsie, bent over her task, singing an Irish ballad. She had hitched up her skirt so that it wouldn't get dirty, exposing the hem of her petticoat.

"There you are. Where have you been?" Marguerite asked. I came out earlier and you were not here."

The young woman stood up and rubbed her back. "I must have been in the latrine."

"You must have been in there for a long time. I saw you leave through the kitchen door and I didn't come out for at least a half hour."

Elsie's face turned red. Marguerite had caught her in a lie.

"You should have had two rows planted by now and you've only just started."

"Where did you find the girl this time?"

Everyone turned at the sound of Madame Peré approaching, hands on her hips.

"When we came out of the house to search for her, she was in the garden," Thérèse said.

"She had completed that much," Marguerite added and pointed to a patch of ground that had been planted.

"Elsie, please come here, at once. I want to speak to you," Madame Peré ordered.

She put down her basket of seeds and joined the women. Elsie's face was as pale as a sheet and her hands were trembling.

"Where did you disappear to when you should have been tending to your chores?" Madame Peré asked.

"I was in the outhouse and then I went to fetch water." the girl's lips trembled.

"Marguerite and Thérèse, did either of you ask Elsie to fetch water?"

The two older servants shook their heads.

"I fetched the water early this morning," Thérèse said.

"Elsie, I do not tolerate lies. When my husband returns home, you will be severely punished."

That will mean a whipping, Thérèse thought. She had never disobeyed her employers, but she had heard of servants who received the whip for being disobedient.

Elsie hung her head.

"Capitaine Peré and I will not tolerate any more nonsense from you," she continued. We have warned you in the past that you are not to abandon your duties and take off whenever you please. If I ever catch you in a lie again, you will be dismissed at once." Madame Peré wagged a finger at the girl. "Capitaine Peré has told me that he will terminate your employment, and you will be forced to look elsewhere for work. I can assure you that no other household in Louisbourg will hire someone who is as irresponsible as you, to shirk your responsibilities to go off doing who knows what. Now, I expect that you pitch in and do your share of the household chores. This is Thérèse's last day with us and when she is gone, I expect that you will carry on with her duties. That being said, I will not allow you into the house until the entire garden is planted today."

Elsie had a stricken look on her face. Planting the garden was a big job that should be shared amongst the servants, and she was expected to do it all by herself.

"Do I make myself clear, Elsie?".

"*Oui*, Madame Peré," she whispered.

"Now, get back to work. There is lots to be done before it gets dark."

Madame Peré turned her attention to Thérèse and Marguerite.

"Look at those lovely blooms over there." She pointed to a lilac bush, over by the fence. "I am pleased to see that they are still blooming after all this time. The people who occupied this house while we were in France must have cared for them."

Madame Peré picked up her skirts and walked over to the fence.

"I would like to give you a bouquet of lilacs as a gift for your wedding tomorrow, Thérèse. They will make a lovely addition to your day."

She bent over and grabbed a bunch of dark purple blooms and handed them to Thérèse. She inhaled their heady sweet fragrance.

"They are beautiful, Madame Peré. *Merci beaucoup*."

"These are for you to carry to the chapel. I am also going to give you two bunches for the table at your wedding breakfast."

"That is very kind of you, to think of me on my wedding day."

"It is my pleasure, Thérèse. Capitaine Peré and I have been pleased with your work as our servant, and my children have benefited from your kind and caring manner with them. My husband and I wish you much happiness and joy as you start your new life."

"*Merci*," she said again.

"Now run along and put those in a jar to keep them fresh for tomorrow, "Oh, by the way, is it this afternoon that you and Monsieur Laserre are to sign your marriage contract?"

"*Oui*, Nicolas and I will be going to the home of Geneviève to sign the contract. It is my understanding that Marguerite and her husband, Gabriel will be joining us there."

"*Oui, très bien*. I will expect you home later this evening."

# Chapter Ten

**Louisbourg, Île Royale, June 1750**

Thérèse woke early the next morning. She looked out the window at a rosy pink sky. It was sure to be a beautiful, sunny day for the occasion. Her wedding day. Her stomach felt jittery, and for a moment she wanted to hide under the covers. Then she thought about Nicolas' tender kisses and his gentle disposition. She had no intention of turning him down, so she ignored the churning butterflies and crawled out of bed. As on any other day, she went through the routine of saying her morning prayers. She fingered the rosary beads and thought about her mother. She would have liked Nicolas, and Thérèse wished that she had lived to help her celebrate her special day. She put the beads in the embroidered pocket she planned to wear and knew her *maman's* spirit would be with her. She thought of other loved ones back in France and wished they too could be with her to celebrate her marriage. She especially missed her *papa*, and she often wondered if she would ever see him again. Thoughts of her family made her feel sad and brought tears to her eyes.

A light tap at the door startled her. She was embarrassed to be seen with a tear stained face and runny nose on her wedding day. She opened the door and let Marguerite into the room.

"I have come to help you dress for your special day. Oh dear, have you been crying, Thérèse? What ever is the matter? You look so sad on what should be a happy occasion for you. Are you missing your family?"

She nodded. Marguerite put an arm around her.

"I understand how you feel. I still miss my *maman* and *papa*, and they have been gone for many years."

She put her *maman's* embroidered pocket down on the bed and took the handkerchief from Marguerite.

"*Merci*. You are such a special friend. I'm so glad I have you. I don't know what I would have done without you today."

"You're a special friend to me too, Thérèse. I am going to miss seeing you everyday. But you will be with your husband and starting a new life with him. All I wish for you is to be happy and healthy together. And who knows, you may have little children of your own one day."

She smiled at the thought of children.

"I thought the mention of children would bring a smile to your face. Now let us get you looking pretty for that new husband of yours."

Marguerite helped her into her wedding outfit, a gold dress with elbow-length sleeves. She tied three sets of ribbons into bows to close the front. An opening at the top of the dress revealed a matching gold stomacher, and a slit at the bottom of the skirt showed off a gold petticoat.

"Now, this cap will look lovely, too. You have such nice thick hair. Try it on."

She placed the white linen cap, trimmed with lace, on her head. There wasn't a looking glass in the room, so she turned to Marguerite.

"How do I look?"

"You are a beautiful bride, Thérèse."

"*Merci beaucoup*," she said as she gave her friend a hug.

Marguerite had brought the outfit to the Peré home a few days ago and insisted she try it on. It had been her wedding outfit, and she wanted Thérèse to wear it on her special day. She touched the light wool fabric and admired its rich gold colour. She did not have a dress for the occasion and was pleased that her friend would lend it to her. Now that the day had arrived, she couldn't wait for Nicolas to see her wearing it.

She touched the cross he gave her when he asked her to be his wife. She had not taken it off since that day.

"Oh, and you need these to complete your attire." Marguerite plucked the bouquet of purple lilacs from the jar of water and handed them to her.

"Now let us go and get you married."

The morning turned out to be a glorious day for a wedding. The sun shone brightly, and the sky was a bright blue, without a cloud in sight.

The little procession started out for the Chapelle Saint-Louis, shortly after sunrise. Nicolas and two of his friends were at the head of the procession. He was dressed in his best suit, and she thought he looked handsome enough to be royalty. He wore dark brown knee breeches, a vest, and a coat, and was crowned with a black tricorne hat. She smiled and gave him a wink when they started up the hill to the King's Bastion. He bought his ensemble at an auction on the quay. It had belonged to someone else, but he purchased it knowing that it was in good condition.

She walked with Marguerite and Gabriel. Marguerite's sister and her family followed behind them.

The chapel was filled with friends and townspeople who wanted to witness the matrimony. The couple stood before the priest and said their vows. She felt a nervous flutter in her stomach as she recited her nuptials. She clutched the bouquet of fragrant lilacs tightly and took a deep breath to calm her nerves. She thought about her *maman* and drew strength from knowing that she was looking over her on this special day. She knew that her dear *papa* would be thinking about her, and that he would remember her and Nicolas in his prayers.

She sighed with relief once she and Nicolas had recited their lines. They were finally married.

Nicolas turned and looked at her with a big smile on his face. Her heart was filled with happiness, and she gave him a big smile in return. He took her hand, and they followed the priest to sign the marriage entry for the parish records.

After morning mass, a wedding breakfast was held for close friends. It was hosted in the home of Marguerite's sister, Geneviève.

She took in the setting when she entered the home. Women scurried about, making last-minute preparations for the meal. The aroma of dishes cooking on the hearth filled the room, and she realized she was hungry.

Geneviève ran up to her and gave her a big hug. "Congratulations! I wish you and Nicolas a happy life together."

Marguerite was next to embrace her.

"You are a special person, and Nicolas is lucky to have you as his wife. I will keep you in my prayers. Do come to visit us once you are settled."

"*Merci*, Marguerite," she said as she returned her friend's hug. "I can't wait for you and Gabriel to visit us in our new home."

"*Oui*, we will come, but you will be busy settling in." She bent over and whispered in her ear. "And you'll be busy doing other things. You know, first there was two and then there was three." She winked, and Thérèse blushed.

Other women surrounded her, congratulated her, and admired her dress. Men wished Nicolas well and patted him on the back. Jeanne and Lucienne, Geneviève's two young daughters, waited patiently to have their turn to talk to her. Both little girls had their mother's chestnut-coloured eyes and dark brown hair.

"You have a pretty dress on," Lucienne said in a soft voice.

"That is a pretty colour," Jeanne said, gently touching her sleeve. "And the material is so soft."

"*Merci*. You both have pretty dresses on today, too."

"*Maman* made them for us," Jeanne said.

The little girls giggled and gave her a slight curtsy. They looked like little miniatures of their mother, with their long navy- blue skirts and matching blue vests over white chemises. Their white bonnets made them look even more grown-up.

"We have something for you," Lucienne said in a timid voice.

"We hope you like it. We made it for you."

"Hush, Jeanne, we don't want to give the surprise away," Lucienne scolded her younger sister.

"Oh, I like surprises," Thérèse said.

Lucienne handed her a floral wreath braided with bunches of blue, yellow, white and pink flowers.

"It is to wear on your head. *Maman* let us go to pick wildflowers so we could make it for you to wear today," Jeanne said.

"It is beautiful. *Merci beaucoup*. I will put it on right now."

She went into the next room where there were no guests and the little girls followed her. She slipped off her linen cap and tucked it into the pocket beneath her skirt. She gently positioned the wreath of flowers on the top of her head and looked at the little girls for approval.

"How do I look?" she asked.

"You look beautiful," they both said. You look like a queen today," Jeanne declared, jumping up and down with excitement.

"I feel like a queen today, with all the attention I am getting. Now come girls, we must not keep the guests waiting."

She took each little girl by the hand and they went back to the wedding gathering.

When they entered the kitchen, she stood and admired the table, decorated for the occasion. Bunches of wildflowers in jars of water adorned the table's white linen cloth.

"What beautiful flowers."

"Guests brought them as gifts for your wedding," Lucienne said.

"Oh, how nice of them. I see someone brought violets, too." She bent over to inhale the fragrance. "They have such a lovely smell."

A gentle hand touched her shoulder and she turned to see Marguerite.

"Come, Thérèse, and sit with your new husband," she said and ushered her to a seat beside Nicolas. He reached for her hand beneath the table and gave it a squeeze.

Père Aubré said the blessing, and then everyone tucked into the food. Thérèse filled her plate with crepes and molasses, baked beans, mussels, bread and cheese. A chocolate cake was served for dessert, with dollops of English cream on top of it. Madame Peré had given Thérèse the chocolate as a gift to serve at her wedding breakfast, and Joseph had baked it that morning in the big brick oven in the bakery. She thought it was the best cake she had ever tasted and declared it to be the best part of the meal.

The wedding party behind them, the newlyweds strolled home, hand in hand, to begin their new life in the little fishing cottage.

She was delighted with her new home. The main room had a fireplace with a cooking hearth. There were hooks alongside the fireplace where she would hang the pots and pans that she purchased with her earnings as Capitaine Peré's servant girl. A set of pewter plates, also purchased, would be placed on the rack above the mantel. There was a wooden table and chairs in the middle of the room where she would place the new linen tablecloth, a wedding gift from Marguerite. A smaller table stood in a corner of the room with fishing gear and playing cards. Nicolas motioned for her to follow him into the room that was to be their bed chamber. The trunk she had brought with her from

France stood in one corner of the room. A table with a candle, an ink well and quill stood under the room's only window.

"What do you think, Thérèse? I built the bed myself."

The four-poster bed had a canopy with matching curtains, made of heavy cotton, to be pulled closed for privacy and to keep out the cold.

"It is beautiful," she gasped.

She had never slept in such a magnificent bed. The cot she slept on at the Peré home was narrow, with a straw mat placed on top of it. She had always assumed that the four-poster canopied bed was reserved for wealthier people, such as Capitaine Peré and his wife.

"What a wonderful surprise! It is magnificent, Nicolas. When did you have time to build it?"

"I worked on it in the evenings, after all the chores were done."

"Who made the canopy and the curtains? I love that colour of green. It will match the quilt that was made for us."

"I had a seamstress make them for me." He put his arms around her and guided her to sit on the edge of the bed. She sunk down into the mattress's softness.

"It is a cloth mattress. The seamstress told me it is not as comfortable as one stuffed with feathers, but it is better than one stuffed with straw," he said, sitting beside her.

"It feels soft and cozy."

He winked at her. "I know. I can't wait to sleep on it with you."

She felt her cheeks get hot. He turned to face her and planted a kiss on her lips. "I think we should check it out right now, instead of waiting," he suggested, continuing to plant kisses on her face and down to her chin.

She giggled. "It is too early to go to bed. Besides, there is work to be done before we sleep. For one thing, the bed needs to be made up before we can sleep in it."

"I don't think I can wait until tonight.

She felt her heart start to race at the thought of being in bed with her husband. She was well aware that couples slept together, but she did not know what to expect in the marriage bed. What did a man do to a woman between the covers, she wondered? She realized that she was soon to discover what it was all about. Nicolas seemed to be unaware of her unease and continued to gently caress her. She was just beginning to relax in his arms when there was a knock at the front door. He continued to hold and caress her until there was another knock.

"Aren't you going to answer the door?"

"*Non*, I am going to ignore it."

"*Bonjour la maison*."

"Go, Nicolas, someone is looking for you."

He huffed and went to the door. She smoothed out her skirts and followed him into the main room.

"Congratulations, Monsieur and Madam Laserre," the men cheered. A group of fishermen stood outside the little cottage holding fishing nets and hooks.

"We have come to let you know that we are heading out to sea to fish for mackerel and herring," one of the men said.

Nicolas scowled at the group. "You don't tell me when you are going on any other day to fish for bait. "Why today? On my wedding day?"

"Just thought you should know. Oh, and by the way, we are short one fisherman. Louis drank too much last night and has a bad headache."

Nicolas groaned. "Well, he deserves it. Just hang on. I will accompany you," he said and stomped away to get his gear.

Thérèse heard the men tittering amongst themselves. "You have the rest of your life to be with your bride," one of the men taunted.

There was no response from Nicolas.

She watched the men walk to the wharf. She shuddered at the thought of her husband rowing a boat through the choppy waves. You better get used to it, she told herself.

"Keep safe, Nicolas," she called after him. He turned and gave her a wave.

She went back into the cottage and looked around. It felt strangely quiet without Marguerite's companionship and the children's chatter. She decided the best thing she could do was to keep busy and started to unpack her belongings. Her life was with Nicolas now and she would make the little cottage into their home.

September 10, 2019

Dearest *Papa*,

I pray this letter finds you and the family in good health. My husband and I have nicely settled into married life. He says I am the perfect fisherman's wife, putting my hand to whatever needs doing on the property. He has been eager to teach me about the dry cod fishery, and he says I am quick to catch on. Our days are full, and we don't get a moment's rest until we collapse in bed, exhausted.

I spend most of the day outdoors, and one of my jobs is to tend a large garden, enclosed with a palisade. We grow enough vegetables and herbs for ourselves and the fishing crews. There is a chicken coop on the property with a rooster and fifteen laying hens. I visit the chickens each morning to collect the eggs, and I am greeted with a variety of squawks and fluttering of feathers. Nicolas has shown me how to milk the goat, Nannie, and she and I have learned to tolerate each other. I was clumsy at first, but over time the task became easier. If time in my day permits, I spend it down on the wharf helping the shore crew. When the cod are unloaded from the shallops, the heads and entrails are removed, and the backbone is cut so the fish can lay flat. This is a job I have not tackled. I have had a sensitive stomach this summer, and I feel nauseated from the smells and sights of the fish being gutted. I prefer to help wash the fish after they are salted. We get the best price from a perfectly white cod, so we need to remove any excess salt, blood spots and blackness that may have been left behind where the backbone has been cut. I help to stack the fish into piles to squeeze out any moisture. When they are ready for the drying process, we place them on the flakes where they are exposed to the sun and wind.

I had a pleasant surprise one morning in July when I opened the door to find a grey and white cat looking up at me, as if she was asking to be invited in. The cottage was invaded by mice, so I decided to let the cat in to hunt them down. I named her Miss Kittie, and she and I have become the best of friends. She spends her nights prowling the property, and in the morning, she heads into the cottage to curl up in her favourite chair by the fire. She frequently leaves us presents outside the door. I usually let Nicolas go out first, but occasionally I go outdoors before him and the unpleasant sight of a dead bird or squirrel greets me. We were delighted when Miss Kittie had a litter of kittens. Marguerite came for a visit a few days ago and brought the three older Peré children with her. Anne was delighted with the kittens and begged Marguerite to let her take one home. We gave into her wish and allowed her to take one.

Give my love to my brother and his family. You are always in my prayers.

Your affectionate daughter,

Thérèse Louise Daccarette

# *Chapter Eleven*

**Louisbourg, Île Royale, 1755**

A child's cry. Thérèse looked around to see who was crying. It was not one of her little boys. Two-year-old Philippe toddled along beside her, his little hand tucked into hers, and baby Pierre snuggled in a sling fastened around her shoulder. She and the children were on their way to let Nicolas know that the noon meal would be ready shortly. He was talking to the shore workers down at the wharf who were salting and stacking cod into piles. When she got closer to the men, she saw a little girl perched on top of an upturned boat, her face contorted into a fierce scowl.

"*Bonjour*, little one. Are you missing your *maman* and *papa*?"

The little girl let out a piercing scream at her approach. She looked to be about two years old, the same age as her son. Her clothes looked shabby and in need of a wash. She wore a long faded blue dress that had myriad stains on it, and a white bonnet covered a tangle of wavy brown curls.

"Do not be frightened, little one," she soothed, putting her free arm around the child. "My little boys and I will not hurt you."

She was puzzled. Where was her mother, and why had she been left unattended? Just then, a tall man rushed to the little girl's side.

"Marie-Louise is my daughter. Please do not frighten her, Madame. She is blind. Strange noises and voices make her afraid."

The little girl stopped crying and she put out her arms saying, "Up *papa*." The man scooped her up and gave her a big hug. Thérèse stood by and watched the man. She noticed how gentle and kind he was with the child.

Nicolas walked up from the wharf to join them.

"Thérèse, I would like to introduce you to Monsieur André Belliveau."

"*Bonjour*, I am pleased to meet you," she said.

Monsieur Belliveau's clothes were worn and tattered, too. His knee breeches had been patched in several places and his once, white chemise was a faded grey. His face was drawn and his eyes had a pained look about them. Where had he come from and where was the child's mother?

"Monsieur Belliveau approached me this morning asking if there was work to be had, and I have hired him to assist the shore workers."

The man set the little girl back down on the upturned boat and she started to wail again.

She was about to ask where the little girl's mother was when Nicolas said, "Monsieur Belliveau, my wife can care for your child."

"*Non*, Monsieur Laserre, my daughter would be terrified to stay with strangers. She has never been apart from me or her beloved *maman*."

The man had a sorrowful look on his face, and she thought she saw tears at the corners of his eyes.

"And I'm afraid the children might hurt her," Monsieur Belliveau continued. "Boys play so rough and Marie-Louise cannot see to protect herself. She will be safe where she is sitting."

"What a pretty name you have. And what pretty curls you have," Thérèse said.

"*Oui*," Monsieur Belliveau agreed. "She is the spitting image of her beloved *maman*, God rest her soul."

So, the little girl had lost her mother. No wonder the poor child was so upset.

"My wife is experienced with caring for children and I have confidence that she will make every effort to make sure that no harm comes to your daughter. The child will be a lot safer in the house with my wife to care for her needs than if she sits on that boat all day. How do you expect to get your work done if you are keeping an eye on your daughter?" I beg you to consider my offer."

"*Oui*, Monsieur Laserre, if you wish that your wife cares for my little daughter, I will obey your command."

Thérèse felt a flip flop in the pit of her stomach. She was uncomfortable about caring for the child. She did not have any experience caring for someone who could not see. Could the child walk on her own? What if she bumped into something in the house and hurt herself? Worse yet, what if she fell on the cooking hearth and burnt herself? She thought about telling Nicolas that she did not feel confident that she could care for the child. She did not know how to care for her, and thought she might be safer sitting near her father, who knew how to see to her needs. She abandoned the idea when she saw how miserable and unhappy the little girl looked.

"You will need to carry Marie-Louise. She cannot walk yet," Monsieur Belliveau said.

She looked old enough to walk. How was she going to carry Marie-Louise and her own baby? She complied with the man's instruction, picked up the screaming child and hoisted her onto her right hip. Philippe toddled along behind them and they made their way to the cottage.

"Come along with me. and we will go and prepare the noon meal for your *papa*," she whispered in the child's ear."

"*Papa*," the little girl sobbed.

She began to hum a tune that she often sang to her own children when they were distressed, and it wasn't long before the child's sobs subsided. Perhaps the child liked music, she thought, entering her cottage. She settled Marie-Louise on a chair at the table. Pierre had fallen asleep during their walk, snuggled against her chest, in his sling. She tucked him into his cradle and then went to finish the preparations for the meal. She chopped parsnips and turnips, and added them to a simmering pot of broth, hanging on a hook over the fire. While she chopped her vegetables at the table, she watched Philippe at play. He was too young to understand that the little girl was blind, but he wanted to include her in his game. He played with his wooden blocks and stacked them up on the floor.

"What are you building, Philippe?"

"Tower," he said.

Nicolas had taught him to say the word when he played with him last night.

Philippe brought two blocks to the table and put them in front of Marie-Louise, but she just stared straight ahead, unable to see the blocks in front of her. Philippe stared at her with a quizzical look on his face. Wanting her to be part of the game, he took the blocks and put one in each of her tiny hands. She held them, feeling the shapes with the tips of her tiny fingers. The little girl learned about her world through touching and feeling, Thérèse realized. She learned about her surroundings through her other senses. Marie-Louise dropped the blocks on the table with a bang. Thérèse chopped chives and gently waved a sprig under the little girl's nose.

"Ummm, that smells good," Thérèse said.

"Ummm," the little girl repeated.

"Ummm," Philippe chimed in and giggled.

"Umm," Marie-Louise echoed and began to giggle too.

Thérèse couldn't help but laugh, too. She let her hold other textures and let her smell them and the game continued. Soon, Marie-Louise was repeating names of vegetables.

Nicolas came in for his meal at noon, and Monsieur Belliveau joined him to see to his daughter. Before the men began to eat, Nicolas said the blessing over the meal.

"Oh Lord, bless this food to our use and thus to thy service and make us ever mindful of the needs of others. Amen."

"Amen," the others repeated, and the adults crossed themselves before taking their seats.

"What a lovely blessing. It reminded me of the blessing that was said at mealtime in my father's home," Monsieur Belliveau said, seating himself beside his daughter.

Thérèse served steaming bowls of fish soup and bread. The adult conversation stopped abruptly when the children demanded attention. Monsieur Belliveau spoon-fed Marie-Louise, but the little girl was more interested in putting her hands in the bowl to pick out the vegetables.

"Carrot," she said after she fished one out of her bowl.

Monsieur Belliveau stared in amazement at his daughter's pronouncement.

"*Oui*, Marie-Louise, that is a carrot. But no more hands in your soup, please," he said.

Marie-Louise stuck her hand in the bowl once more and her father reached over and gently removed it, wiping her tiny hands with his napkin. The little girl protested, pulling her hand away from her father's grasp and sticking her thumb in her mouth.

Thérèse recounted the details of how Marie-Louise had learned about the smells and textures of the vegetables she had chopped for the soup. Monsieur Belliveau rewarded her with a smile.

"So, that is why she is so adamant about sticking her hands in the soup," he laughed.

After Philippe had finished his meal, Thérèse helped him down from his chair and he hurried off to play. Marie-Louise began to fidget on her father's lap.

"*Non*, you stay here with *papa*."

"Play, *s'il vous plait*," she said.

"You are welcome to put her down on the floor, beside the blocks," Nicolas suggested. "She will be fine sitting there, and she will enjoy playing with Philippe."

"*Oui*," Monsieur Belliveau said as he put her down on the floor to play.

He rejoined the adults at the table, and every few seconds he nervously glanced in his daughter's direction, a terrified expression on his face. Marie-Louise was unaware of her father's distress, and she played contentedly with the blocks, piling them up, one by one, and knocking them down again, giggling all the while.

It was a wonder that Marie-Louise was such a good-natured child, given that her *papa* was so overprotective. It seemed the man had never let the poor child out of his sight before.

After the meal, Thérèse put the children down for a nap on the bed, in the room she shared with Nicolas. Monsieur Belliveau stood up when she re-joined the men at the table.

"*Merci*, Madame. I appreciate your kind hospitality towards myself and my daughter. I must get back to help the shore workers with the salting of the fish this afternoon."

After the door closed behind him, she went to the cradle to attend to the crying baby. She sat down at the table, across from Nicolas, and tucked Pierre against her breast for him to nurse. Sitting in amiable silence, Nicolas lit his pipe, sat back in his chair, and began to unravel the mystery of their newest worker to the fishing station. She listened as he described the fate of Monsieur Belliveau and his child.

"At noon, when the other workers went to their quarters to eat their noon meal, I took Monsieur Belliveau aside and spoke with him so I could learn more about his origins. He told me about his journey to Île Royale. He and his wife, who was with child, and their daughter, Marie-Louise, fled from their home in the Chignecto region of Acadia. I believe the British have renamed the place 'Nova Scotia.' Monsieur Belliveau's younger brother accompanied them."

"*Pourquoi*, Nicolas? Why did they leave?"

"First, Fort Beauséjour was attacked and taken by the British in June of this year. It had been a French post near their village."

"Oh Nicolas," she gasped.

"*Oui*, Thérèse, these are uncertain times for us all."

The baby had finished nursing, and she put him over her shoulder and gently patted his back. She silently prayed for peace, but she knew that the world around them was filled with greedy people who wanted to conquer whatever lands they could. Every time she stepped outside her door, she caught a glimpse of British naval ships anchored off the Louisbourg harbor.

"In July," Nicolas continued, "news reached the Acadians in the Chignecto region that the Nova Scotia Council in Halifax had met with several of the deputies from the surrounding regions on the mainland. The Acadians were advised to swear oaths of allegiance to the British Monarchy or else they were to be deported from their lands that had been home to them for decades. The deputies refused to swear oaths to the British crown and the British imprisoned the men. The council members refused to give the Acadians any indication of how much time they had to make preparations for this departure. When Monsieur Belliveau and his family heard of the plan to force the Acadians from their lands and deport them to places unknown, they were deeply distressed by the news. Fearing for their lives, they made the decision to pack up what belongings they could carry with them and flee from the wrath of the British. They stole away under the cover of night to decrease their chances of being attacked by British soldiers. Their journey took them through the woods, until they approached a landing where a schooner had been secretly arranged to transport Acadians to Île Royale. It was a difficult journey for Monsieur Belliveau's wife. She was with child when they left the Chignecto region and the poor woman started having labour pains on the journey. The women on board all knew it was her time to give birth but when they begged the captain to stop at a Mi'kmaq settlement along the way, where there was a medicine woman to help with the birthing, he refused their pleas for help. He told them that he dared not stop for fear of being spotted by the British. The poor soul bled to death and she was buried at sea."

"Did the baby live?"

"Sadly, *non*, God rest both their souls."

"Oh how sad. No wonder he and the child look so forlorn. Where do Monsieur Belliveau and his brother live?"

"They are staying in a hut on the neighbouring fishing property of Monsieur Desroches. There was an empty building that was not occupied by his hired men, so he offered it to them. Monsieur Belliveau's brother has accepted work with Monsieur Desroches. He needed another fisherman and the young man has fishing experience."

Nicolas stood with his pipe clenched between his teeth.

"I need to see to the workers. The fishermen should be arriving soon with today's catch. I hope they travel safely and can avoid the British blockade. I have heard that they have been capturing fishing vessels and have taken the fishermen as prisoners of war."

She shuddered at the thought of war and snuggled Pierre to her chest and the world was as peaceful as the sleeping babe in her arms.

Monsieur Belliveau came to the cottage after his day's duties were completed. Marie-Louise had fallen asleep after an afternoon of being entertained by Philippe.

"Come in, Monsieur Belliveau, and have a seat," Nicolas said. "Can I offer you a drink of rum?"

He slumped into a chair. "*Non, merci*," I would like to talk to you about a serious matter." He rubbed his eyes with the back of his hand.

Was he crying, Thérèse wondered?

"Do you know if there is a convent in the colony?" he asked.

"*Oui*, the sisters of the Congregation de Notre-Dame run a school for girls. It is located on the point," Nicolas said. "Why do you ask?"

"I would like to request that you give me a bit of time off tomorrow to go and visit the sisters."

"What for?"

"I am going to ask them to take in my daughter. I do not believe that I can care for a blind child on my own, especially as she gets older."

Tears glistened in his eyes and a sob caught in his throat. "I cannot look after her like a mother can, and she needs constant care that I cannot give her. The child has never had her eyesight. She was born that way. The only option I have come up with is seeing if the nuns would care for her. It would break my heart to part with my little daughter, but I pray the nuns would give her a good home. She is all I have left. But what choice do I have?" He wiped his eyes with the sleeve of his chemise.

"You are thinking of giving her up permanently?" Nicolas asked.

"*Oui*," he whispered.

Thérèse was stunned.

"Perhaps my wife could look after the little one during the day while you work, and you could take her home with you at night," Nicolas suggested. "You could still be with her in the evenings."

Monsieur Belliveau smiled, but then he frowned again.

"I could not accept your kindness, Monsieur Laserre. You and your wife have your own children to care for."

Thérèse's heart went out to the man. She could not imagine the pain he must be feeling. First, to lose his wife and baby and now his daughter. That would be too much to bear.

"I would be pleased to care for Marie-Louise. She is such a good-natured child."

"But I do not know how I could reciprocate."

The three of them sat in silence. Finally, Monsieur Belliveau spoke again.

"Could I do odd jobs in the evenings to repay you for your kindness?"

"That sounds like a fair exchange," Nicolas said. "There are many jobs that need doing. You could chop and split firewood, clean the chimneys, tend to the garden and animals. Thérèse already has her hands full looking after the house and the children, so an extra pair of hands to do those jobs would be a big help to us."

"Merci beaucoup, Monsieur Laserre. Just give me a list of chores that need doing, and I will get to them after my regular work is done for the day."

"You can call me Nicolas, just as the other fishermen do."

"Then you can call me André."

With the issue settled, Marie-Louise spent her days with Thérèse and the boys. The little girl seemed to thrive in Thérèse's care and was happy to be with other children. André proved to be a big help around the property, and Nicolas was pleased with his work. When he came to collect his little daughter in the evening, he beamed with pleasure when he heard about her day.

At first, Thérèse thought Marie-Louise was small and frail for a two-year old child. She tried to have her do sedentary activities by placing her in a chair at the table. She thought the dirt packed floor was rough for her to crawl around on, so she spread out a quilt with toys to keep her occupied while she worked. The little girl could hear Philippe roaming about the room, and it wasn't long before she crawled off the quilt and followed him around. The first time she went near the hearth, Thérèse panicked.

*"Non,* Marie-Louise, the hearth is hot. There is a fire on the hearth, and I do not want you to burn yourself."

"Hot fire," the little girl repeated when she snatched her up and plunked her back down beside the toys. She removed the pots and pans from their hooks beside the fireplace and arranged them around the edge of the hearth stones to prevent the child from getting to close to the fire. Marie-Louise continued to explore her surroundings but every time she neared the fireplace, she said "hot fire" and moved away. She felt around the room's furnishings and could soon pull herself up by holding onto chairs. One day, after Thérèse had completed the breakfast dishes, she had an idea. She took Marie-Louise by the hand and asked Philippe to take the other one.

"Hold on tight," she said and the three of them walked round and round the room.

At first, it was as if she and Philippe were carrying the little girl.

"Now, put one foot in front of the other," she instructed.

Marie-Louise cautiously moved her left foot.

"That is the right way," Thérèse encouraged. Now, move your other foot. That's it. Now, do it again. Move one foot, then the other foot."

Holding on tightly, Marie-Louise repeated the movement several times.

"That's good. You are walking, Marie-Louise." She bent down and gave her a big hug and the little girl squealed with delight at her accomplishment. Philippe was enjoying the parade too and the children continued to walk around the room, with less success. Marie-Louise fell on her bottom twice and after several attempts the children lost interest in the game.

Marie-Louise took her first step on her own a few days later. Her father had finished his work for the day and just arrived at the cottage to pick her up. Thérèse bent down and took the little girl's hand. The two of them walked hand in hand toward Monsieur Belliveau when, suddenly, Marie-Louise let go of Thérèse's hand. She took a step by herself, lost her balance, and plopped on her bottom. Before Thérèse could help her up, she had stood up and on tottery legs took a step forward, then another one, until she reached the waiting arms of her father, who smiled with pleasure.

October 15, 1756

Dearest *Papa*,

I pray you and the family are keeping well. I talk of you often to my husband and my little sons. I am teaching Philippe and Pierre to say their prayers, and we include you on our prayer list.

My little sons are growing quickly. Philippe had his fourth birthday, and he is so much like his *papa*. He spends all of his time down on the wharf, watching the men at work. He loves to fish, but he is too young to go to sea with the fishermen, so he pretends by hanging a fishing line over the edge of the wharf. Pierre is sixteen months old, walking and learning to say a few words. The first word he could say was "*papa*," and the second one was fish. I think I am going to be surrounded by a house of fishermen.

The conflict between Britain and France sounds grim. We receive bits and pieces of news from vessels that manage to escape the British naval blockade in the harbour. André Belliveau, one of the shore workers is from Acadia, a colony occupied by Britain, tells us that the British have forced thousands of men, women and children from their homes. Entire villages were burnt to the ground, and their lands pillaged. The people were loaded onto ships, bound for places unknown. Monsieur Belliveau had family still living in Acadia, and he thinks it is unlikely they escaped the deportation. His parents were getting on in years, and they were feeble. He fears that they may not be able to survive a long journey on a ship. He had married siblings with children and many aunts and uncles with families of their own. He does not talk about it, but I can see by the look in his eyes that he is grieving for loved ones he may never see again. My heart goes out to him, and I have added him and his little daughter to my prayer list.

In September, a devastating fire destroyed the King's Bakery, which supplied bread for the Louisbourg garrison. Nicolas and other men from the town helped to battle the blaze. He and his hired men came home hours later, exhausted, covered in soot and smelling of smoke. The four bakers lived above the bakery–they lost their home, and the artillery storehouse was also destroyed. The commercial bakers in town and the bakery at the King's Hospital have taken over the task of baking bread for the soldiers.

I must close for now so I can deliver this letter to the quay, to be sent on the next ship to France.

Your affectionate daughter,

Thérèse Louise Dacarette.

# *Chapter Twelve*

**Louisbourg, Île Royale, September 1757**

Thérèse stood at the window to watch a shallop with her husband and two of his hired fishermen row away from shore. Two other boats had oared out ahead of theirs. She watched the scene until all three vessels had disappeared behind a curtain of thick fog. She knew that her husband would not have taken such risks during peacetime, but there was a blockade of British naval ships blocking the harbor, and he felt that the heavy fog banks would protect the fishing boats from an attack. Many French vessels had been seized, with cargo and their crews taken into enemy hands. She shivered at the thought of her husband being taken as a prisoner of war. She touched the wooden cross at the base of her neck and prayed for the safe return of him and the other fishermen. He was anxious to get his catch of cod before St. Michel's Day, which was at the end of the month. He also hoped to catch enough fish to supply his family for the winter.

Throughout the day, the wind picked up speed, and the ocean became a tempest, crashing violently against the rocky banks. Could a little fishing boat survive those big waves, she wondered? She hoped the men would make it back to Louisbourg soon. It was starting to rain, and they would be soaked to the skin, catching their death from cold if they did not make it safely to shore.

She jumped at a knock at the door. It was André Belliveau. When she let him in, the wind gusted around him and threatened to snatch his tricorne hat off his head. Rain dripped from his already wet clothes, making puddles on the dirt-packed floor.

"*Bonjour*, Madame Laserre, I have come to inform you that one of the shallops has returned. They were afraid of getting caught out at sea and came in before they had reached their quota of fish for the day."

"Was my husband among them?"

"*Non*, I am afraid not, Madame. Let us hope they will arrive soon. The storm is getting worse. The other shore workers and I have gathered up the fish flakes and put them inside the shed. We have decided to stop work for the day and will be retiring to our quarters early. Since your husband and the other fishermen have not returned from sea yet, is there anything else we can do for you?"

"Have you put the piles of cod that were salted yesterday in the shed as well?"

"*Oui, Madame*. Is there anything else we can do for you before we retire?"

"*Non, merci*. You have done all that you can. I pray that the men arrive home soon."

"*Oui*. me as well. It looks like it is going to be a wicked storm."

"*Oui*," she nodded, feeling terrified at the thought of her husband and his hired fishermen out in that wicked weather.

Five-year-old Marie-Louise ran to her father and stretched out her arms for him to hug her.

"Can I come home with you now, *papa*?"

"*Non*, little one, you must stay here, where it is safe and warm. I will come for you tomorrow, after the storm has passed."

"*Papa*, I will miss you," she cried.

"I will miss you too, my precious daughter, but I want you to stay here with Madame Laserre so you can keep Philippe and Pierre from getting into mischief." He gave her a kiss on her cheek and hugged her tightly. "Now you be a good girl and do as I say."

"*Oui, papa*."

Monsieur Belliveau stepped out into the storm, promising to return when the weather changed.

The children were irritable, and nothing Thérèse did comforted them. After tucking them in to bed for the night, she stood at the window, watching and hoping to catch a glimpse of the fishing shallops returning. The evening dragged into night, the wind howled mournfully, and torrents of rain lashed against the window, making it impossible to see through the glass. Finally, she gave up her post and slumped into a chair. She clutched her rosary beads tightly in her hands and prayed for the men's safe return while the storm raged on and on. She should be doing some mending to keep her hands busy, but her mind and heart could not focus on that task. The later the hour, the more fretful she became. Darkness had fallen, and there was still no sign of the men. The fire had died out and she began to pace the room to keep herself warm. She prayed they had seen the storm coming and had made for the nearest shoreline to wait it out, but her worst fear was that they might have been swallowed up by the sea's rolling waves. She reached for her prayer book to calm her quivering nerves. The room was quiet, and the only light came from the candle on the table. She was soon comforted by the word of God.

"*Maman*, what is the matter?"

She was awakened at a light tug on her sleeve. Philippe stood beside her chair. She must have dozed off while reading her prayer book last night. She was shocked to realize that it was morning already. She looked out the window to a dull grey sky. The storm must have passed in the night. With a sinking heart, she remembered that her husband had not returned home. He was still out there somewhere.

"What is wrong, *maman*?" Philippe asked again.

"There is nothing wrong, my child. Now go and wake up Pierre and Marie-Louise while I stoke up the fire for breakfast."

She did not want to worry the children unnecessarily, in case her husband and his hired fishermen had waited out the storm in the safety of a sheltered inlet. Philippe did not leave his mother's side but continued to stare up at her with sad eyes.

"Where is *papa*? He did not come home last night."

"*Non*, he did not."

"Where is he, *maman*?"

"Perhaps he decided to wait out the storm before trying to make it back to Louisbourg," She tousled her son's hair. "Now go on and wake up the other children. They will be hungry and want their breakfast."

She went about her morning routine of washing her hands and splashing cold water on her face. She felt stiff and sore after a long night of sitting on a wooden chair. She prepared breakfast for the children, who ate up plates of bread and cheese before starting their daily chores. When they were completed, it was time for play. The boys headed outdoors to collect the eggs from the hen house, and Marie-Louise helped her in the cottage to wash up the breakfast dishes.

Thérèse did not feel hungry. In fact, she felt nauseated, so she hung the kettle over the hearth to boil water for a cup of mint tea. Perhaps the hot drink would settle her stomach. It didn't help that she was frightened for her husband's safety. She had heard of fishermen who lost their lives at sea. Could this be her husband's fate too? She hoped not, and she prayed that he would come through the door at any moment.

Monsieur Belliveau arrived later that morning to check on Thérèse and the children.

"It was a wild storm yesterday," he said.

"Did your brother make it home safely from sea?" Thérèse asked.

"*Oui*, his shallop made it back before the wind and rain picked up. All Desroches's men made it back safely. The Desroches property suffered damage. There were boats overturned, and two of them were smashed to pieces. They were fortunate that the buildings weathered the storm. Where is Nicolas? Have the boats returned?"

"*Non*," she shook her head.

"Monsieur Belliveau nodded.

"I will go and check the property for damage. On my return, I will bring you a load of firewood. You will need it. There is a chill in the air today."

"*Merci*," she said, head bowed so he wouldn't see the tears in her eyes.

She was petrified, certain that something terrible must have happened to her husband and the other fishermen. She wiped her eyes with her handkerchief and turned back to the table, where she had left Marie-Louise kneading the dough for bread. The little girl hummed to herself while her small fingers worked the dough.

She put her arms around the child. "You are doing a good job, Marie-Louise." She tried to keep her voice from quivering.

Marie-Louise had proved to be a big help with house chores, although she was blind. She enjoyed having the company of a little girl, and it almost seemed like she was her own daughter.

There was a loud rap on the door. Thérèse jumped. Her heart thundered in her chest, and her legs trembled. Three of her husband's hired fishermen entered the cottage. She clutched her cross tightly. *Mon Dieu,* where was Nicolas? Why wasn't he with them? The men were silent and had somber looks on their faces. Something was terribly wrong. She began to tremble all over, and her legs felt as if they were going to give way beneath her. A chair was placed in front of her, and she slumped onto it.

"Madame Laserre," Louis, the taller of the three, began, "we have just returned and must let you know that your husband and the other two men in his shallop did not return with us. We headed northeast up the coast to avoid any British naval ships. We lost track of the other fishing boats when the wind came up. We were all tossed about so badly that it was all we could do to keep the boat afloat. We were fortunate to get into the shelter of an inlet, out of the wind. We put down anchor and waited out the storm. This morning, we headed back southwest, along the coast to Louisbourg and north of the lighthouse, along the shore, we saw the wreckage of a shallop. We went closer for a better look. The vessel had been tipped upside down and smashed up against the rocks. There was no sign of the bodies."

"*Non, non*, not my dear Nicolas," she wailed.

She sat with her head down. She could not bear to look up and see the stricken looks on the fishermen's faces.

Then a thought struck her. Perhaps it wasn't her husband's shallop. She lifted her head to look at the men.

"How do you know it was the boat that Nicolas was in? There could have been other fishing vessels out trying to get in a catch before the end of the season."

"We think that the men were trying to catch a goodly number of cod and were not keeping an eye on the weather. When the wind came up, they were probably trying to make a run for Louisbourg. The wind caught them and capsized the boat. We examined the wreckage and recognized Henri's favourite cloak washed up on shore. It would have come off when he fell in the water," Louis said.

"How do you know it was his cloak?" she exclaimed.

"There were two initials sewn into the fabric and they were H for Henri and L for Luc."

"Her eyes filled with tears, and a sob escaped from her throat. She lowered her head and let the tears fall. How could it be true that he was dead? He promised to always be careful when he was out at sea.

"May God be with you and your children, Madame Laserre," Louis said.

Her head jerked up at the mention of her children. Where were they? She frantically looked around the room, for fear they would be gone from her too. When she saw Philippe and Pierre standing near the door, she stood up and went to them. She hadn't heard them come in. They must have seen the fishermen coming to the cottage and followed them to the door. She held them tightly against her chest. Marie-Louise appeared at her side and she included her in their embrace, the unmade bread forgotten on the table. She cried tears for her children, who had just lost their father, and she ached for the loss of her beloved husband.

"What is wrong, *maman*?" Pierre asked.

Her heart ached at the thought of telling her youngest son that his father was dead. How could she tell him? He was too young to understand death.

"*Papa*," she began slowly, "has gone to heaven to be with his *maman* and *papa*."

Pierre and Philippe looked up at their mother. Tears streamed down their faces.

"Why?" Pierre cried. "Doesn't *papa* want to be with us anymore?"

She was at a loss for words. What could she tell a three-year-old child to make him understand his *papa* was never coming back?

"Your *papa* loves you very much, Pierre, but God wants him to live in heaven now." She smoothed the top of his head.

"Does that mean we will never see *papa* again?" Philippe asked.

"*Non*, Philippe." she whispered. "You will see him one day when you go to heaven."

Louis approached the little group, and she released the children. He cleared his throat.

"Madame Laserre, we hired men will help you and the children in any way we can."

She felt so numb that she could not think of what needed to be done.

"Madame Laserre, I am going into the town. Is there anyone in Louisbourg who you would like to have with you at this time?" Jean, the smallest of the fishermen, asked.

"*Oui*," A sob caught in her throat. "Could you go to the Peré home and give Marguerite Pineau the news?"

"*Oui*, Madame. I will give her the sad news of your husband's passing. Would you like me to go up to the Chapelle Saint-Louis and inform the priest?"

She could only nod.

The rest of the day passed in a blur for her. Marguerite arrived and took over the running of the house and provided comfort to her and the children. André visited often and stepped in to do jobs that might otherwise have been done by Nicolas. News spread quickly and by the next day, friends and neighbours arrived bearing gifts of food and expressing their condolences. Nicolas had been well-liked by everyone who knew him. Merchants, tradespeople, seafaring captains and fishermen alike rallied round Thérèse and the children to let her know how much they appreciated his kindness and loyalty towards them. Nicolas had made many friends in the community and was well known throughout the colony. The hired fishermen and shore workers who worked on his fishing station liked and respected him as their employer. Throughout that day, she heard many comments from her husband's hired men that he had been a fair and trustworthy employer.

She woke early on the day of the funeral. Rousing from what little sleep she had, she remembered the events of the past few days and wished it had only been a bad dream. Unfortunately, it was not a nightmare that she could put out of her mind. This morning was the funeral mass for her husband and the two fishermen who had been with him in the boat. Rising from under the covers to the cold, damp room, she felt nauseated. The bile rose to her throat, and she snatched up the chamber pot from under the bed. The tears slid down her cheeks while she emptied her stomach's contents into the pot. She wiped the tears away with a cloth and splashed her face with cold water from the wash basin. She wondered how she would manage to make it through the day. Would the nausea pass? Could she be brave and stay strong without breaking down in tears? She had been feeling nauseated for a few days and suspected the pregnancy was upsetting her stomach. Perhaps a cup of mint tea would be soothing. She decided to go to the main room to stoke the fire, to boil water.

The funeral mass was to be held in the little military chapel in the King's Bastion Barracks. The procession started out from the Laserre fishing property, led by the clergy, with an assistant at the front, carrying the cross, the curé and the mourners following behind. Thérèse felt numb, walking directly behind the curé. She just kept moving forward, putting one foot in front of the other. She was vaguely aware of her friend, Monsieur Belliveau, at her side, gently coaxing her to keep going. If he hadn't been there to guide her, she might have just stood in the middle of the path, unaware of what was happening around her. The clergy recited psalms and she tried to comfort herself by focusing on the chanting, but her mind seemed unfocussed. Her dear friends, Marguerite and Gabriel, accompanied by the children. The procession passed the soldiers on guard duty at the Dauphin Gate and wound its way along the quay, until they turned onto Rue Toulouse, the street that would take them up the hill to the King's Bastion Barracks. Entering the chapel, she took her place beside her children. The strong scent of incense permeated the room and made her feel queasy and light-headed. She had nothing to hold onto, so to comfort herself she took both of her sons' hands and held on tight, willing herself to make it through the mass. She had been on the verge of tears all morning and made sure that she had a clean handkerchief in her pocket. When the funeral ended, the procession filed out of the chapel. She took up her spot behind the clergy, who lead the way to the town's cemetery to view the cross, erected in memory of Nicolas. Monsieur Belliveau stepped up beside her and gently took her arm to help her along. She was pleased to see many familiar faces among the parishioners, waiting to make their way out of the chapel.

She crawled into bed, exhausted that night. The stress and grief she felt had drained her, but sleep would not come. She reflected on the events of the day and the people who attended the funeral to pay their respects. She was touched to see that her old employer, Madame Madeleine Peré was among the mourners. It was even more surprising to see Madame Drucourt, the most prominent lady in the colony, the Governor's wife. She felt blessed to live in such a caring community.

# *Chapter Thirteen*

**Louisbourg, Île Royale, November 1757**

Thérèse sat by the fireplace. It had been Nicolas' favourite armchair, and she pictured him in it now. Pipe in hand, a big grin on his face, laughing at something funny one of the children said. Her needle moved swiftly through the wool of the stocking she was darning for Philippe. She sighed heavily. Her mending wasn't helping to relax her, and it felt as though she carried the worries of the world on her shoulders. What was she to do about the vase? And the toy soldiers the boys were playing with? What if another child was missing them? Where had Soldat Bouchet found them? Had he purchased them? Or were they also a mystery that she needed to solve? Then he had brought the bottle of wine. How could he afford to purchase such luxurious gifts? The vase certainly looked familiar. She was certain it was the same pattern of porcelain and markings as the vase that belonged to Capitaine Peré and his wife. Was Monsieur Bouchet under Capitaine Peré's command, she wondered? Could he have stolen the items from an officer's home? How? When? If they were stolen goods, she did not want them in her home. She did not want to be accused of thievery. She had to do something, but what? Who could she talk to? Could she go to Père Aubré? She could confide in him. Or should she pay a visit to Capitaine Peré's home to discuss the matter with him? If she did, would he accuse her of stealing? She prayed that he would not think that she was the culprit. The more she thought about the situation, she knew what she had to do.

The next morning dawned brisk and cold. She bundled herself and the children up in their warmest clothes. It was the winter fishing season, and everyone had to pitch in to salt and dry the cod. She was glad that her remaining workers decided to winter in the colony to help with this season's catch. The fishermen went out each day to catch the fish, and the shore workers prepared the fish for market. Monsieur Belliveau was shore master and supervised the processing of the fish. She went out each day to oversee operations and to make sure there was a pure white quality of cod, with no blood stains or black marks remaining. On days when they were short-handed, she pitched in to help process the fish, but it was difficult with three children under foot. After she spoke to Monsieur Belliveau and asked if he could mind the children for a couple of hours, she walked into the town. She pulled her hood over her head to keep out the wind and headed off at a brisk pace.

She knocked at the kitchen door of the Peré home. Marguerite still worked for the family and let her in.

"*Bonjour*, Thérèse. Come in. You must be frozen."

She stepped into the familiar kitchen and pulled her hood off.

"It is so good to see you." She gave her friend a big hug and kissed her on both cheeks.

"It is wonderful to see you too. Where are the children?"

"Monsieur Belliveau is watching them. He'll have his hands full, given all the questions Philippe and Pierre are bound to ask him, so I won't stay long."

"What brings you by today?"

"I would like to speak with Capitaine Peré. Is he available to speak with me?"

Marguerite's eyebrows rose. "Non, he is up at the guard house. Madame Peré is home."

"I will have a word with her."

"I will let her know you are here." Marguerite scurried away to find her mistress.

A few minutes later, Madame Peré bustled into the kitchen.

"*Bonjour*, Thérèse, how are you?"

"I am doing as well as can be expected, Madame Peré," She said and curtsied. "It was kind of you to attend the funeral for my husband and his hired fishermen."

"It was the least I could do for you and your children at this difficult time. You will always be well thought of in the Peré household. The children speak of you often."

"How are the children?"

"They are all fine. The boys have grown and are no longer living in the home. They have followed in their father's footsteps and have been recruited to be cadets of the Compagnies franches de la Marine. Jean has joined a company in Montreal and Paul is at Québec City."

"Where have the years gone? The boys were children when I worked for you and Capitaine Peré."

"*Oui*, Thérèse. It seems like it was just yesterday when they were babes in arms."

"How are Anne and Madeleine? Where are they today?"

"Anne and Madeleine are doing well. They attend the Congregation of Notre-Dame school for girls. Capitaine Peré and I decided that Madeleine was old enough to attend this year, and she loves it, especially since she can sit with her older sister."

"Would you like coffee, Madame Peré? Would you like coffee, Thérèse?" Marguerite asked.

"*Oui*, Marguerite, please prepare some refreshments for our guest."

Thérèse smiled at the thought of chatting over a hot drink with her friend.

"May I speak to you in private for a few moments, Madame Peré?"

Marguerite's eyebrows rose again. She was surely wondering why her friend wanted a private word with her mistress.

"*Oui*, Thérèse, let us go into the parlour."

She followed Madame Peré into the next room. She glanced around and did not see the vase that she used to dust. She felt frozen with fear. Where had it gone?

"What is it, you would like to discuss with me, Thérèse?"

Her mouth was dry, but she found her voice and explained her visits from Monsieur Bouchet, the gifts he brought and her suspicions about their whereabouts. She removed the vase from the sack and handed it to Madame Peré.

"I thought you had a vase that looked similar to this one, but I do not see it here today."

Madame Peré studied it.

"Turn it upside down and look at the markings on it. I recognized those markings as being the same as those on the vase I dusted for you."

"*Oui*, you are very observant. I still have the vase. It is in my bed chamber. I will go upstairs, and we can have a look at it."

She watched Madame Peré hustle from the room and heard her retreating footsteps on the stairs. She breathed a sigh of relief that she still had it. She was glad it hadn't been stolen.

"*Oui*, it does have the same markings on it," Madame Peré said when she returned. She turned the vase over and showed it to her.

"*Oui*, it does," Thérèse agreed.

"I just remembered that one of the other officer's wives mentioned that items kept disappearing from their home. I am sure she said that one of her vases disappeared. The officer had *soldats* working in his home and was not sure who had taken the items."

"Does she have children who would play with toy soldiers?"

"The couple have a son and two daughters. The daughters also attend the Congregation of the Notre-Dame school. I do not know how old their son is, but it is possible the toys belong to him."

Thérèse nodded. She felt sick at heart. She knew that Soldat Bouchet would be severely punished if he was the thief, but she did not approve of dishonesty either.

"I would like to show the vase to my friend. She should be able to tell me if it is hers. I will also speak with my husband regarding this matter. He will know how to handle the situation. I will ask him to speak with you once he knows what the circumstances are."

"*Merci beaucoup*, Madame Peré. You are most kind to help me."

"*Oui*, Thérèse. I appreciate your honesty."

"Refreshments are served," Marguerite announced poking her head around the corner of the door.

Thérèse went to the kitchen to enjoy the rest of her visit with her friend.

She felt relieved to have discussed the issue with Madame Peré. Now, all she could do was wait until Capitaine Peré let her know what he had found out.

# *Chapter Fourteen*

**Louisbourg, Île Royale, December 1757**

Thérèse sat quietly. A single candle danced and flickered in its brass candlestick holder. The only sound in the room was the embers hissing and crackling in the fireplace. She stared at the prayer book that remained closed, on the table, in front of her. It was Christmas Eve, and she thought it was the loneliest and saddest Christmas of her life. She desperately missed Nicolas. It was already three months since his death, but she could still not believe he was gone. She wished for a miracle and for him to come back to her and the children. Perhaps he was stranded on an uninhabited island and was waiting to be rescued. It was unlikely, but it was worth wishing for.

She wondered about her family, across the ocean in La Rochelle and prayed for them. Was her father keeping well? Were her brother and his family all healthy? Would they all be celebrating Christmas together? She had not received a letter from anyone in her family for several months. The last letter had arrived in the spring, on a ship that managed to enter the harbour before the British blockaded French waters. She dearly missed her family at this time of year. She often thought of her mother and wished that her two little boys could have met their grandmother. They would have adored her. But she thanked God daily for the children's health and the joy they brought to her life.

She knew how disappointed the boys would be to not have any special Christmas foods prepared for them this year. She prayed that their meager food supplies would keep them and the other colonists fed through the winter. She not only had to worry about the boys, but also the child she was carrying. The colonists had received rations of salted meats, flour, butter and vegetables for the past few months. Royal officials had further rationed the flour supply and ordered that each family get a portion that was one-third flour and two-thirds rice. This was to be used to make bread. There was plenty of salted cod. She had grown a large garden in the summer and had a supply of root vegetables and dried herbs stored away. She and her children would be eating plenty of fish soup and stew this winter.

She prayed for her family's safety. If rumours proved to be true, that the British were planning a full-scale attack on Louisbourg, and if ships were wintering in the port of Halifax so they could get an early start on their mission in the spring, she hoped she could protect her little family. She dreaded the thought of war. She could not understand why nations wanted to conquer new lands when there was so much loss and destruction.

The thought of war reminded her of Soldat Bouchet. What would happen to him if he was found guilty of theft? She wondered if she made the right choice in going to visit Madame Peré to divulge her suspicion that he had given her stolen goods. Could this have consequences for her and the children? If he learned that she had questioned the vase's whereabouts, could he come after her or the children?

She sighed. Weary of dwelling on her worries, she picked up her prayer book and began to read.

*Tap. tap, tap*. Her head came up from her reading. That was a familiar knock. What was Monsieur Belliveau doing at her door at this hour? Wouldn't he be going to midnight mass? She put the prayer book back on the shelf and hurried to let him in.

"*Bonjour*, Monsieur Belliveau. What brings you to my door at this hour?"

He entered the cottage, bringing with him a cold breeze. He was carrying Marie-Louise, her shawl wrapped tightly around her.

"*Joyeux Noël*, Madame Laserre! Marie-Louise and I have come to get you and the boys to join us at midnight mass."

She had decided not to attend midnight mass this year and had sent her children off to bed, much to their dismay.

"It was very kind of you to think of me and the boys, but we are not going this year. I put the children to bed, and they are already sleeping."

"*Pourquoi*? Why not? You told me that you planned to attend the mass tonight."'

"I changed my mind."

"*S'il vous plait,* please come," Marie-Louise begged.

"*Oui,* we would like you and the boys to come. It is Christmas Eve, Madame Laserre. Why don't you wake the boys and join us at the mass? Marie-Louise and I would enjoy your company."

"*S'il vous plait,*" Marie-Louise persisted.

Thérèse's heart melted at the little girl's request, and she agreed that she and the children would accompany them. She enjoyed Monsieur Belliveau's company and appreciated his thoughtfulness during these difficult times. He, too, must be lonely this evening, remembering Christmases past with his wife and other loved ones who were lost to him. Why hadn't she considered his feelings instead of just focusing on herself?

She woke the little boys. It would be a long walk to the Chapelle Saint-Louis, so she bundled them into warm clothing. The children were excited to be going out on an adventure, and they were thrilled to spend time with Monsieur Belliveau and their little friend. They dawned their long cloaks, put up their hoods, and headed out into the night. Big fluffy snowflakes fell, and the ground underfoot had a layer of powdery snow. They crossed over the wooden drawbridge at the Dauphin Gate and passed groups of soldiers, standing guard. Entering the town, they met up with other people going to midnight mass. At first, Marie-Louise wanted to walk with the boys. Pierre and Philippe walked on either side of her and took her by the hand to guide her so she wouldn't fall in the snow. When she got cold, her *papa* picked her up and carried her. Thérèse was pleased to see how kindly the boys treated and helped the little girl whenever they could.

The little group followed the people making their way through the town and up the hill to the King's Bastion Barracks, to the military chapel. The scent of incense filled the little church, and she was reminded of Nicolas's funeral. She silently choked back sobs and settled herself among the other parishioners to celebrate the birth of Christ. Candles were alight in holders along the walls to brighten the room, and evergreen boughs were scattered around to make the chapel festive for the occasion. Staring straight ahead, she focused on six candles that had been placed to illuminate the picture of the Patron Saint Louis. A nativity was displayed in front of the altar.

"Look, *maman,* there is the *crèche,*" Philippe said, pointing to the nativity.

The carved wooden figurines of the holy family and several carved animals stood in a mound of hay, and their shelter was a stable made of bark. Carved figures of the shepherds and wise men crowded around them, bearing gifts for the Christ child.

The blessings and the music that were sung during the Mass lifted her spirits. She was glad Monsieur Belliveau and his daughter had encouraged her and the boys to attend with them. Before the mass ended, she followed the congregation to the altar rail, where she knelt to receive Holy Communion. She was disappointed when the mass ended so quickly. The tranquility of the chapel had relaxed her, and she felt peaceful. She reluctantly filed out with the rest of the parishioners.

People wished each other *Joyeux Noël*. Soldat Bouchet appeared at her side and her heart quickened. Did he know she had taken the vase to Capitaine Peré's home?

"Merry Christmas, Madame Laserre. How are you and your children managing?"

"*Très bien.*" She didn't offer any more information.

Had the officials started an investigation or had the matter been dropped, she wondered?

"How are you celebrating the holiday?" he asked.

"We enjoyed mass and will go home and celebrate with some singing."

"That sounds wonderful."

Perhaps the matter was to be resolved in the new year. He did not give her any indication that he knew she had gone to the authorities to question the vase's origin.

Monsieur Belliveau joined Thérèse and scowled at Soldat Bouchet.

"Pardon, Madame. I'm off to the tavern for a meal," he said and faded into the crowd of people walking down the hill.

She and Monsieur Belliveau walked in silence. She was glad when he didn't mention the encounter. Running into the soldier had dampened her mood, and she didn't feel like talking.

People vacated the King's Bastion, chatting cheerfully to each other. Their voices had a merrier ring to them, their worries temporarily forgotten. Thérèse ushered her little family through the crowd. Parishioners lit candles and torches that twinkled brightly against the night sky. This was a tradition she remembered from her childhood in France, and the scene made her nostalgic. She remembered walking home from the church with her family, carrying candles and singing Christmas carols. Somewhere in the crowd, a rendition of "Les anges dans nos campagnes" echoed through the air. Monsieur Belliveau carried Marie-Louise and sang softly to her. Thérèse was moved by the singing and joined in, too. Soon, everyone around them was singing. She loved music, and the joyous mood around her lifted her spirits. The wind picked up and the snow continued to swirl around them, but no one seemed bothered by the weather. Trudging along through the snow, they sang "Adeste Fideles." When the song ended, Marie-Louise clapped her hands together. Pierre and Philippe joined in the applause.

"*Papa*, could you sing "Minuit, Chrétiens" to me," Marie-Louise asked.

"*Oui, ma petite chérie*." Townspeople joined in until, slowly, one family after another dropped off as they reached their homes. The children continued to sing merrily until the group reached Thérèse's cottage. The adults' singing had petered out, and they listened to the children in companionable silence.

"Would you and Marie-Louise care to join us for a meal before you go home?" Thérèse asked when they reached her door. "I don't have any treats for the occasion, but I can offer boiled salted cod and vegetables."

"Marie-Louise and I will accept your invitation. At least the food will fill our bellies and we will enjoy your company."

"The boys and I will enjoy your company too."

She went into the cottage, took off her cloak and stoked the fire to start preparations for the meal. Monsieur Belliveau and the children stood close to the hearth to warm themselves. She had just added wood to the fire and looked up from her task when she heard two familiar voices entering the cottage.

"*Joyeux Noël*, everyone."

Thérèse hurried to hug Marguerite and Gabriel. "*Joyeux Noël*. It is so good to see you both. We just returned from midnight mass."

"Gabriel and I were at mass too, but we did not linger to talk with others. We went straight home to gather up food to bring to you and your family."

"You brought food? You did not have to do that," Thérèse said.

"We most certainly brought food. We wanted to share the Christmas celebration with you, and we did not want to come without bringing treats. My sister sent you two meat pies that were prepared in her bakery today. She also sent along apple tarts for desert, and there is enough for all of us."

"I am the carrier of the flour," Gabriel said. "Geneviève had an extra sack of flour and she wanted you to have it. She was worried that you might be running short."

Gabriel tossed the sack of flour down on the floor.

"It is so kind of Geneviève to think of my family, and it is so nice to be able to share the occasion with both of you," she said, giving Marguerite another hug.

She took the meat pies, placed them in *tourtière* pans and prepared to bake them on the hearth. She reached into the fire with her ashes shovel and brought out hot coals to place underneath each pan. Then, she put hot coals on the lid of each pan so the pies would bake evenly.

Gabriel excused himself and stepped outside the door. He returned seconds later with a Yule log and presented it to the children. It was a huge birch log that would keep the room warm for most of the night.

"Do you know why we burn the Yule log?" he asked.

"The log is placed on the fire to honour the gift of light that the Christ child brought to the world," Pierre answered.

"*Oui*, you are right. Your *maman* and *papa* must have explained that to you," Gabriel said to Pierre.

"We are celebrating the saviour's gift of light to the world," Philippe volunteered.

"I want to feel the log," Marie-Louise asked, as she she put out her little hands to feel it.

"It's big," she said.

"*Oui*, it is, Marie-Louise. Pierre, can you help me by pouring rum over the log?".

He took the bottle of rum Thérèse retrieved from the cupboard. She saw the bottle of wine that Soldat Bouchet had brought as a gift still sitting on the shelf.

"That is the bottle of wine Soldat Bouchet brought *maman*," Philippe blurted.

She cringed and glared at Philippe. Monsieur Belliveau scowled. It was the same look on his face that she had seen when he encountered the soldier in her home a few weeks ago, and the dismayed looks of the other adults in the room did not go unnoticed.

"What was he doing in your home?" Marguerite asked.

"I've heard that he is a thief," Gabriel said.

No one spoke for what seemed like moments. Finally, Gabriel broke the silence.

"Come children, let us prepare the Yule log for the fire."

Thérèse sighed with relief when the subject of the soldier was dropped.

They all crowded around to watch the ritual.

"In the name of the father, the son and the Holy Ghost," Gabriel prayed, holding the log securely in both hands.

Pierre tipped up the bottle of rum and poured it over the log's surface. Gabriel carefully placed the log on the fire, and everyone was fascinated to watch the alcoholic contents cast a beautiful blue hue to the flames.

Marguerite pulled her aside when the others were eating. "Be careful, Thérèse, I've heard that the soldier who has been coming to visit is trouble. I wouldn't be letting him in if I were you. I'm glad Monsieur Belliveau checks in on you and the children. He is a good man to have around the property."

Thérèse knew Marguerite's predictions about Soldat Bouchet were probably accurate, but she silently prayed the accusations weren't true.

The rest of the night was spent companionably, enjoying the festive occasion of eating, singing and telling stories. It was almost dawn when the company left for their own homes. Marguerite and Gabriel left first, promising Thérèse they would visit again soon to see if there was anything they could do to help her during the long, cold months ahead. Next, it was Monsieur Belliveau's turn to leave. He woke his little daughter, who had fallen asleep on his lap. Thérèse watched him bundle her up for the walk home. She noticed how gentle and caring he was with the child. She wondered if he wished for the tender loving care of a mother for Marie-Louise. She appreciated the thoughtful acts of kindness he did for her. He kept her woodpile stocked and often brought her game when he went hunting, so she and the children would have fresh meat. She wondered what she could do to return his kindness. Then she noticed that his mitts were threadbare. She still had wool left and could knit him and Marie-Louise a new pair of mitts. She would give them as little gifts when they got together for New Years.

*It had been a wonderful Christmas,* Thérèse thought as she watched her friends leave. She felt truly blessed to have such caring and loving friends. It had been a respite for all of them to share in the celebration of Christ's birth, and she prayed that Christ's love would help to carry them through the months ahead.

# *Chapter Fifteen*

**Louisbourg, Île Royale, January 1758**

"Thérèse," a man's voice echoed against the wind.

She looked up from the fish she was piling up with the shore crew to see Capitaine Peré approaching. Her heart quickened. Was he coming to give her news about Soldat Bouchet? What had happened to him? The breeze whipped at her shawl, and she pulled it tighter around herself.

"*Bonjour*, Capitaine Peré." She gave him a slight curtsy. "What brings you out this way?"

"I would like to speak with you privately, if you can spare the time."

"*Oui*, I have time. Please come with me," she said and led him into the cottage.

The children sat huddled by the hearth. Philippe and Pierre were singing "Alouette" to Marie-Louise.

"I will pluck your feathers off your nose, I will pluck them off your head," Philippe sang, touching Marie-Louise on the nose and then on her head. The little girl giggled.

The children stopped their singing when Thérèse and Capitaine Peré entered the room. They looked curiously at the man who had come into the house with their *maman*.

"Children, can you please go in the other room for a few minutes so I may speak to Capitaine Peré?"

"*Oui, Mamam.*" The boys said, getting to their feet and heading for the bed chamber. Marie-Louise followed behind them, feeling her way around the edge of the hearth, until she hit the wall that led to the other room.

"Have a seat by the hearth to warm yourself," she offered.

"*Merci beaucoup*, Thérèse."

She pulled up a chair and sat across from him. She was nervous, and her heart continued to thud in her chest.

"I dropped by to thank you for coming forward with the vase. Monsieur Bouchet is under the command of my good friend and colleague, Capitaine De Ganne. He had ordered three of his men to repair the fence around his garden, and do maintenance inside the house. Soldat Bouchet was one of the men ordered to work for him. Capitaine De Ganne's wife started to notice personal possessions missing and was devastated when her most cherished piece of porcelain was gone. Capitaine De Ganne said that when his men were questioned, none of them admitted to stealing the items. When I brought the vase back to the De Ganne home, his wife recognized her cherished piece and he decided to have the barrack room of his men searched. We suspected that the thief was Soldat Bouchet, since he does have a disreputable reputation. But we couldn't be sure it was him until all three men were searched. Under his mattress, we found a stash of stolen goods. Fishing hooks, decks of cards, you name it, it was there."

"Ah, so he *had* taken fishing hooks from the table when he visited, shortly after my husband's loss," she explained.

"We found a time piece that had engraved initials on it. It read, "MD." The Capitaine recognized that it was his, and this confirmed that Bouchet was the culprit."

She put her hand over the cross that hung at her neck. "How could he be so deceitful? He came with toy soldiers for my little boys. Would you know who those belong to?"

"*Oui*, Thérèse, Capitaine De Ganne has a five-year-old son. They are his."

She was anxious to get rid of any stolen goods out of her home. "You can give them back to him. Oh, and then there was a bottle of wine that he brought. It's sitting on my cupboard, unopened," she said.

"Thérèse, Capitaine De Ganne has told me that you may keep the wine and the toys for you and your children. These are items you can keep as gifts. It is the couple's way of thanking you for your honesty. Madame De Ganne is grateful to have her treasured vase back."

"Please thank Capitaine De Ganne and his wife for me. What will happen to Soldat Bouchet?"

"He has been suspected of many thefts over the years and has gone before the Conseil de Guerre, who have decided that he will serve a prison sentence for the winter months. Unfortunately, for you, he will be released in the spring. We will need all hands to man the place, if the British attack."

She was relieved that he would not be executed, but she did not like the thought of him coming around again to bother her and the children either.

"It was very kind of you to drop by and give me the news."

"It was my pleasure, Thérèse. I must be taking my leave," he said rising from his chair. If there is ever anything you need, just let me or my wife know."

"*Merci beaucoup*, Capitaine Peré."

# Chapter Sixteen

**Louisbourg, Île Royale, April 1758**

"Ships," Philippe exclaimed, bursting through the door. "I see ships coming, *maman*."

Thérèse put down the spoon she was using to stir the soup and hurried outside with the boys. The colonists were eager to see ships arriving with supplies, and more soldiers to help defend the place. Packed ice had blocked the harbour for most of March, barring ships from arriving. Now that the coast was clear, vessels could safely make their way into port. She scanned the horizon for white sails. Her heart sank when she spotted them. She could just make out that they were British ships. Not another blockade, she groaned. Now, French vessels would certainly not be able to make it to Louisbourg. Would they attack this year? She hoped not, but it was inevitable that it was going to happen.

Philippe and Pierre jumped up and down, excited to see the ships.

"Do you see them, *maman*?" Pierre asked.

"*Oui*, I do. Those are British ships, boys."

"They are? How do you know, *maman*?" Philippe asked.

"They are flying the British flag. Do you see the red, white and blue criss-crosses fluttering in the wind?"

"*Oui, maman*."

She turned and walked back to the cottage, no longer interested to see the ships. The thought of another summer with meager food supplies was upsetting. How was she to keep her family alive with so little food to eat? She walked slower these days. She was big with child and she felt it kick her.

She busied herself, adding more logs to the fire and stirring the soup.

She was just about to call the boys in for the noon meal when they burst through the door with Monsieur Belliveau and Marie-Louise.

"*Maman*, you should see what Monsieur Belliveau brought us."

She looked from the boys to Monsieur Belliveau. "What is it?"

"*Bonjour*, Madame Laserre. I have been out hunting and brought you and your family a grouse."

She eyed the plump bird and her mouth watered for fresh meat. She and her family had lived on salted cod all winter.

She smiled. "That was so kind of you. *Merci beaucoup*. It will be a welcome treat."

"There will be plenty of meat on that fowl. It is a big one, and you will get several meals out of it."

"When did you go out hunting?"

"I went out yesterday. I shot a grouse for my family, too."

"Did you take Marie-Louise?" She couldn't imagine taking a little blind child into the woods. She would be so afraid she would get lost.

"*Oui*, I did. I took her to meet my Mi'kmaq friends. They were delighted to meet her, and she stayed with them while I went hunting."

"I didn't know you were friendly with the Mi'kmaq around these parts."

"*Oui*, I have met them many times when hunting in the woods. I can speak some of their language. Where I come from in Acadie, the Acadians are friendly with the Mi'kmaq. I grew up among their people. Oh!" he smiled at Thérèse and put Marie-Louise down on her feet. "I have gifts for you and the boys."

"More gifts," Thérèse said.

"*Oui*," Marie-Louise clapped her hands, "and they are nice and soft."

Monsieur Belliveau pulled three pairs of moccasins out of his sac. Two pairs for Philippe and Pierre, and a pair for Thérèse. She took the pair he handed her to caress their soft leather and admire the beadwork on them.

"They are beautiful. Did your Mi'Kmaq friends make them?"

"*Oui*, I brought them tobacco and traded with them for the moccasins."

"Look at mine." Marie-Louise held up a footed moccasin.

"Yours are beautiful too, Marie-Louise. They have pretty coloured beads on them, just like mine.

Philippe and Pierre put their moccasins on and danced around the room in them.

"They will keep your feet warm and dry, boys." Thérèse told them.

*"Oui, merci beaucoup,* Monsieur Belliveau." Philippe and Pierre said.

Monsieur Belliveau and Marie-Louise stayed for the noon meal of fish soup and bread. When the children had finished eating, Thérèse gave them permission to go and play. When they left the table, Monsieur Belliveau had a serious expression on his face.

"What is it?" she asked.

"I will be joining the militia this spring."

She gasped. That meant he would be caught up in the fighting if the British Army attacked the colony.

"My brother and I, and many others in the community, will fight alongside the soldiers if the British Army lands on our shores. We could be getting our orders any day now."

She cringed at the thought of war. What about Marie-Louise? What if something happened to her *papa*? A sob caught in her throat.

"I am hoping to stay within the fortifications to be close to you and the children. I want to be close by so I can protect you against any danger. You and your children mean a lot to me."

Her heart skipped a beat and she was moved that he thought a lot of her and her little boys.

"I appreciate your kindness and friendship, and the boys are very fond of you and Marie-Louise."

"When the time comes and I get my orders, would you take care of Marie-Louise for me? Could she live with you? I could be away at all hours of the day. She means the world to me." His eyes filled with tears. He reached for his handkerchief and wiped them away. "If there is an attack by the British and something happens to me, would you take care of my little girl?"

His eyes filled with tears again and she felt them brimming in hers too.

"Of course, I love the child as if she were my own. She will always have a home with my family."

He reached over and gently touched her hand.

"You are a special person, Thérèse."

His touch stirred something inside her, and she felt her cheeks flush with excitement. Did she like the attention or was she just feeling embarrassed?

"I would be pleased if we could drop the formalities. I would like you to call me André." He smiled at her. She smiled back.

"And I would be pleased if you would call me Thérèse."

# *Chapter Seventeen*

**Louisbourg, Île Royale, June 1 - 8, 1758**

The wind blew and the sea had a rough surf. Thérèse pulled up her hood and tucked her cloak more tightly around her. She pulled up Pierre's hood and he yanked it off. She reached to put it back on, but he ran to catch up with Philippe. He was becoming more independent and she missed the days when she could cuddle him. He had turned four in April, and she gave him his first pair of knee breeches and shirt. Philippe turned six in March and was growing like a weed. He had outgrown his clothes, and she made them over for Pierre. He was thrilled to wear grown-up clothes and took great pride in keeping up with his older brother.

She and the children entered the town and joined the procession that wound through the streets before arriving at the Chapelle Saint-Louis for morning mass. It was a feast day and people were dressed in their best clothes to celebrate the Octave of the Corpus Christie. It was a more somber occasion this year. People's thoughts were on the threat of attack by the British. She heard murmurs of "ships" and "British" and "sails" coming from all directions. Was there a new development that she wasn't aware of?

André approached after morning mass. He carried Marie-Louise, who sobbed uncontrollably in his arms.

"What is the matter, *ma chérie*?"

She reached out to take Marie-Louise from André, but the little girl kept her face buried in her *papa*'s chest.

"I have distressing news, Thérèse. The British fleet are here in full force. There have been reports that there are over 70 sails bobbing around in Gabarus Bay. As soon as the weather clears, I fear they will attempt a landing."

She reached for her cross. "*Mon Dieu*! Please, not war."

André nodded. "I have been given my orders and must leave Marie-Louise in your care."

"*Non, papa*, please don't go! Please don't leave me behind."

"I can't take you with me. It is just too dangerous for you to be with me. Now, I want you to stay with Thérèse. She will take good care of you."

He kissed the top of her head and put her down. She continued to cling to him.

"*Papa* has to go now, but I want you to help Thérèse take good care of Philippe and Pierre. I will be back soon to check on you."

"Don't go! Please don't go, *papa*," the child wailed. Tears slid down her cheeks and her nose ran.

Thérèse pulled out her handkerchief and crouched down to dab at Marie-Louise's face.

"How about coming home with me? You and I will make French toast for the noon meal. It will be our treat on this special day. I even have maple syrup that I have been saving for such a special occasion."

Marie-Louise's head came up and she gave Thérèse a flicker of a smile.

"That sounds delicious, doesn't it, Marie-Louise?" André asked.

The little girl nodded.

"Now, you are going to have to help me up, before I fall down, Marie-Louise." Thérèse reached out a hand but it wasn't Marie-Louise who took it. André helped her up and gave her hand a gentle squeeze. They looked at each other for a moment until Thérèse broke the silence.

"Would you like to join us for a meal?"

"*Non*, I must be off. I have received my orders to help man the battery on Rochefort Point, but I will be inside the fortifications."

"Please take care of yourself," she pleaded.

"I will. And you take care of yourself, too. I think you should be planning to move into the town. You and the children will be safer inside the fortifications. You should be making arrangements for a place to stay," he said. "You cannot stay on your property much longer."

She nodded.

"Capitaine Peré and his wife have invited me and the children to stay with them in their home. Marguerite will be staying in the home as well. She does not feel safe living in the house on the waterfront. Gabriel will continue to operate the forge. He will be kept busy repairing the munitions that will be needed." She brushed a wisp of hair off her face.

"Does Capitaine Peré know you will have another child in your care?"

"*Mais oui*, I have told him that Marie-Louise will be with my family."

"I am glad those arrangements have been made. I will know where you are. Do you think the couple will mind if I visit you and the children at their home?"

"I don't think they would mind if you come to see your little daughter."

"I will see you soon, then. *Au revoir*, Thérèse." He touched her arm gently.

"*Au revoir, ma petitte*." He bent down and gave his daughter one last hug, and then he was gone. The little girl started to whimper again.

Thérèse was turning off Rue Talouse, onto the quay, when she heard a familiar male voice. Oh, *non*, why did she have to run into him today? She turned to face him.

"*Bonjour*, Soldat Bouchet."

"How are you, Madame Laserre?"

"I am fine. The children and I were just at morning mass."

"I have just been let out of prison. I have been in that cell since last December. The officials searched my belongings and found items under my mattress. They assumed I stole them, but it was my roommate who was stashing his loot under my mattress."

She did not believe he was telling her the truth, but she let him ramble on.

"It sure feels nice to see the light of day again. They let me out because they need every able body to man the place."

He smiled at her. "I have something for you." He took a hat from under his arm and gave it to her.

"Why are you giving me a man's hat?" she asked.

"It could be your husband's hat, and I thought you would want it."

She gasped. "My husband's hat? How did you get it?"

"I was visiting a tavern last night, and the fellow sitting across from me explained that he found a hat washed up on the shore, north of the lighthouse. He showed me the initials embroidered on one of the folded corners. I cannot read, but he told me that they are N. L. The fellow did not want to give me the hat, but I told him that if I won our card game, he would give it to me."

She looked at the hat and, sure enough, "N. L." was stitched in green thread on one of the folded corners. She remembered doing the stitching a few days after she had settled in the little fishing cottage with Nicolas. She hugged the hat close to her chest and fought back tears.

"I don't believe that gambling is appropriate behaviour in the eyes of God, but I appreciate your thoughtfulness in giving the hat to me. It is a treasured possession that I can pass on to my sons. I am glad you will be able to do your duty for the King and colony, but I do suggest you pay a visit to Père Aubré and seek penance. *Au revoir*, Monsieur Bouchet," she said and turned on her heel to hustle the children home.

Later that afternoon, she slipped out of the cottage while the children were entertaining each other by singing songs. She walked down to the wharf and sat on the edge of its rough boards to look out over the water. The wind was strong and created huge waves. She hoped the weather remained miserable, so the British army couldn't make a landing. No attack by the enemy meant that she and her family were safe. She wished the rough surf would chase them back to wherever they came from, but she knew that sooner or later they would attack Louisbourg.

She took her husband's hat out of her pocket and looked at it. The colour of it was faded, and the felt was worn in places. She smoothed out the folds and thought of Nicolas. His love of music. The joy of having two sons. And his passion for adventure out on the sea. The sea that had taken him from her. She realized that the hat was a sign to let her know that he would not be coming back to her. He would never again walk through the door of their cottage with a string of fish in hand. She knew that she must let go of her fantasies and accept that he was gone. But she could never love anyone else but him. She could move on and face whatever atrocities came her way, but she would do so as a widow. She could not think of re-marrying and allowing another man to take his place.

She spent much of her time preparing for the move into town. She mended holes in the boy's knee breeches, darned stockings and folded each child's clothing inside blankets. She made Marie-Louise a new skirt out of one of her old wool ones and sewed her a new chemise out of some leftover linen she had used to make diapers, dresses and little caps for her unborn babe. She knew that her time was drawing near, and she suspected the birth would occur within the next couple of weeks. She dug into her trunk and brought out the baby blanket the boys were swaddled in and put it to her cheek to feel its softness. It smelled of lye soap and lavender. Would it be another boy, or would she be blessed with a daughter this time? She thought of Nicolas and remembered him telling her that he hoped they would have a little girl one day. A lump formed in her throat. She pushed it down and kept herself busy. She bundled the baby clothes into the blanket and put it aside with the children's bundles. She reached into the trunk again and brought out the skirts and petticoats she had worn before her pregnancy. She would be nursing the infant, so she pulled out the chemise that fastened in the front. She put her mother's embroidered pocket aside, so she could put it on. She decided to wear it to keep it safe and to have her *maman's* presence near. The last item to come out was a stack of letters from her father. She added them to her bundle and tied the corners of the blanket into a knot.

On June 8th, she woke early. She was lying on her back. When she tried to sit up, her back hurt. She eased up slowly and swung her legs over the edge of the bed. She stood up and rubbed the small of her back. She ran her hand around to her belly and felt a sharp kick from the baby. She felt tired and wished she could stay in bed, but she had no choice but to get up, see to household chores and care for the children. She went to the main room and stoked up the fire to chase the chill away. She sat down with her prayer book and began to pray. She fingered the smooth beads on her rosary and prayed for God to keep her and her family safe. When she stood up, she realized she needed to use the outhouse. She slipped into her shoes and stepped outside into the fresh morning air. It was a glorious day. The sun shone brightly, and the sky was a brilliant blue with not a cloud to be seen. Her spirits lifted and she felt more peaceful than she had in days.

Her happiness was shattered a few hours later when an officer arrived at her door.

"*Bonjour*, Madame Laserre, I am Lieutenant Duval. I have orders from the Governor for you and your family to vacate the premises. Madame Peré has asked me to help you move into the town today."

Her heart sank. This was not good news. He continued.

"Madame, the British troops landed this morning."

"Where did they land?" She hoped it wasn't close to her property.

"They landed at Anse de la Cormorandiere."

"Was anyone killed?"

"The British side lost many men. Some were shot. Others drowned when their boats capsized in the surf. We figure we lost around a hundred men. The French retreated back to Louisbourg, but the troops who were camped further east along the shore were blocked by the enemy. We assume they were captured and taken prisoners of war. Capitaine Peré was among four officers who has not returned."

Her heart went out to the Peré family. War did dreadful things to people. Madame Peré must be frantic with worry for her husband.

"You are ordered to leave your property today. You must pack your belongings at once. Bring what you can get in carts. Whatever is left will be burned."

"*Pourquoi*?" she exclaimed. What do you mean, burned?"

"Governor Drucourt has ordered all buildings outside the walls to be burned so the British army cannot occupy them."

"*Non,*" she protested. "I will not allow it. This is my property and I forbid you to burn my buildings. My husband worked hard to build up this business and I won't allow it to be destroyed," she cried. She shook with rage and her heart hammered in her chest.

"Madame, you do not have a choice in the matter. All of your neighbours and everyone around this area is receiving the same order."

"I will stay here and defend my buildings, and no one can stop me." She stomped her foot on the dirt packed floor.

"*S'il vous plait,* Madame. I beg you! Think of your children. They would not be safe here."

The officer was right, and she knew it. She was not thinking rationally. The children must be her first priority. She choked up and could not speak. Tears streamed down her face and she nodded.

She turned away from the lieutenant and saw the terrified looks on the children's faces.

"I'm scared, *maman,*" Pierre cried. Marie-Louise began to cry too.

"*Non, maman,* I do not want to go. I want to stay here," Philippe sobbed.

She bent down and drew the children close.

"We are going on an adventure, to live in a new house where there will be other children to play with."

The children continued to sob.

"Won't it be nice to have other children to play with?"

All three shook their heads.

"They might play games or have toys that you have never played with before. Does that sound like fun?"

The children continued to sniffle, and she dabbed at their faces with her handkerchief. She was devastated by the news, and she was at a loss to know how to console the children. She remembered that the lieutenant still stood in the doorway. She stood up, sighed and faced him.

"I understand how difficult this must be for you and your children, Madame Laserre. What can I do to help you?"

She was surprised by the sympathy in his voice.

"Can you give me an hour or so to gather what we need? I will go and fetch the carts that are over by the shed."

"Allow me to do that for you. You have enough to do. I will bring the carts around to the door for you."

"That is kind of you. *Merci beaucoup*. We will have everything by the door when you return."

She had all the clothes and personal belongings that she was taking with her ready. They just needed to be loaded into the carts. What was she missing, she wondered as she looked around? She walked into the other room. She looked at the barrels and coils of rope. What about the food that was left? She would take it with her and contribute it to the Peré household.

She went back to the other room and found the children still crying. She bent down and put her arms around the three of them.

"Now, I want you to be brave for *maman*. I am sad to be leaving too, but we will be safe where we are going. Everything will be all right. Just wait and see. Now, we must hurry and not keep the lieutenant waiting."

The children were solemn and looked up at her with big sad eyes.

"Boys, can you go to the shed with Lieutenant Duval and bring back all the salted cod that will fit in the carts?"

They nodded and silently slipped out the door.

"Marie-Louise, can you help me gather up the food that we will take?" She took the little girl by the hand and they set to work collecting flower, brown sugar, salt, dried peas, dried herbs and vegetables. They filled sacks and stacked them by the door.

Once the food was ready to go, she gathered up the few belongings that she had packed and put the bundles by the door. She looked around at her home, and sadness overwhelmed her. There were so many memories of Nicolas in this little cottage. She could not bear the thought of it being destroyed. She walked into the bed chamber and looked at the bed where she had lain with him and where their children had been conceived. She picked up the quilt that had been given to them when they were married. She walked back into the main room where she retrieved the brass candlestick holders from the table. Her eyes blurred with tears. She tried to blink them away so she could see the home that she had spent many wonderful hours with her family, but they kept coming. She looked at the chair by the fireplace where he used to sit, smoking his pipe. The chair on the other side of the hearth, where she sat many an evening rocking the babies to sleep or helping to mend nets. She glanced at the table where her family ate their meals, and across the room to the cupboard that held the earthen wear dishes and mugs. She was shocked to realize that she had forgotten to pack her prayer book and rosary beads. She picked them up and wrapped them up in the wedding quilt with the candle stick holders.

"*Maman*, the lieutenant is back with the carts," Philippe said.

"Did you go to the shed and get the cod fish?"

"*Oui, maman*, it is in the carts."

The noise of their belongings being stowed in the carts jolted her back to the present. She wiped her eyes, hoisted up her skirts and stepped outside of her home for the last time.

"Do you have everything you need to take out of the house?" Lieutenant Duval asked.

"*Oui*," she said.

"If you can handle this cart, I can take the other one," Lieutenant Duval said.

"*Oui*, I can. Marie-Louise, you can walk beside me and hang on to the edge of the cart."

Pierre let out another piercing cry.

"What is wrong, Pierre?" she asked, walking over to check on him.

"*Maman*, what will happen to the chickens and all the baby chicks? They will be lonesome without us," he blubbered. "And what about the goats? We can't leave them behind either."

"Do not worry about the chickens and the goats. I will see to it that they are brought into the town," the lieutenant assured Pierre.

"*Maman*, what about Miss Kitty? We can't leave her behind," he wailed.

Her heart ached for her child. He loved all the animals.

"Miss Kitty will be able to take care of herself. She knows how to stay away from danger."

"But I will miss her, *maman*."

She put her arms around him and gave him a hug. "I know you will miss her, but we can't take the time to find her. We must hurry to get into the town, where it is safe."

Just then, a little grey and white cat appeared at Pierre's side.

He picked up the cat and she purred in his arms. "*Maman*, can I take her? *S'il vous plait*."

"You may take her with you as long as Madame Peré will allow you to keep her in the house."

Pierre nodded and cuddled the cat.

She returned to where the lieutenant waited. "*Merci*. You have been most helpful, and I appreciate your patience."

Lieutenant Duval smiled.

"Thérèse, I smell smoke," Marie-Louise said.

"I know. I do too."

The sky around them was hazy with drifting smoke from neighbouring properties, and Thérèse's eyes stung. She saw a group of soldiers heading in their direction and heard the lieutenant barking orders at them. Her buildings were to be demolished next. She cringed at the thought of losing her business. Tears stung her eyes again, and she found it hard to see where she was going. She pulled out her handkerchief and dabbed them away. She felt empty inside. First the death of her beloved Nicolas, and now the loss of her home and business. What was she to do?

The journey to the Peré home was an arduous one. All her muscles ached from being tense, and her back throbbed. She wished she could lie down in the middle of the path and rest her weary bones. Some inner strength urged her to keep moving, so she put one foot in front of the other and kept pushing the cart forward. Up ahead, she saw the gate, guarded by groups of soldiers. It was a majestic entrance to the town, she thought as she maneuvered the cart onto the drawbridge and over the cobblestones. Its coat of arms, carved into the gate's archway, welcomed people into the town. She and the children would be safe behind these walls.

She was thinking they would soon be there when she felt a piercing pain in her belly. She had been getting pains lately, but this one was so sharp she wondered if it was her time. It couldn't be. She thought she had a couple of weeks until her due date.

"What is wrong, Thérèse?" Marie-Louise asked.

She must have heard her gasp.

"Nothing is wrong, just catching my breath."

She was thankful when the pain subsided and sighed with relief when they reached the Peré home.

Marguerite greeted them at the door and gave Thérèse a hug. She began to cry again. The day had just been too much, and she broke down in her friend's arms.

"Everything will be all right. You and the children will be safe here," Marguerite assured her. She released herself from Marguerite's embrace to rub the small of her back.

"Thérèse, you look done in."

"I am. I need to sit down. My back is aching."

"Oh goodness, Thérèse. Here is a chair. You sit down and rest. That must have been a long walk for you in your condition. The children and I will see to unloading the carts."

Madame Peré hurried into the kitchen to speak with Lieutenant Duval. Her face was ashen, and her eyes were red and puffy.

"*Merci beaucoup*, Lieutenant Duval," she said in a composed voice. We appreciated your help today."

"It was my pleasure, Madame. He walked over to speak to Thérèse. I am going back out to your property to see to the enlisted men. I will see that your animals are cared for."

Thérèse remembered her manners. She stood up and gave him a slight curtsey. "*Merci beaucoup*. I apologize if I was short with you when you arrived at my home."

"I accept your apology. We are all feeling the strain, and I understand that you would be upset about leaving your property." He smiled at her and then turned to address Madame Peré.

"I will be back when I have news for you."

Two little girls hurried into the kitchen. Anne, the oldest of the two, squealed with delight when she saw Thérèse. Anne, now eight years old, was tall for her age and walked with the same graceful air as her mother. Madeleine was six and hung back when she saw the people in the kitchen.

"My, how you have grown since I saw you last! You were just a wee baby when I lived with your family."

Madeleine nodded and gave Thérèse a shy smile.

Thérèse's children were introduced to Anne and Madeleine.

"Why are her eyes closed? Is she sleeping?" Madeleine pointed at Marie-Louise.

"Madeleine, do not point your finger at someone. That is rude behaviour, and I will not tolerate it in this house," her mother scolded.

Marie-Louise moved closer to Thérèse's chair and she put an arm around the child.

Marguerite took Madeleine aside. "Marie-Louise is blind. She cannot see like you can, but I want you to be nice to her. I'm sure she would like to be included in your play. Perhaps you can show her your dolls."

Madeleine nodded.

"Now, come along children, and help me unload the carts," Marguerite said.

Just then, Miss Kitty made herself known to the household by jumping out of Pierre's arms. She flew out the open door before he could catch her. The children hurried after the cat and brought her back into the house. Pierre looked at Thérèse.

"Can we keep her here, *maman*?"

Thérèse looked at Madame Peré. "Pierre did not want to leave without his favourite pet. Would you mind if he keeps it here?"

"*Oui*, he may keep the cat, but I do not tolerate animals on the table or furniture."

"*Merci*," Pierre said as he hurried out the door to catch up with the other children.

"Thérèse, I will show you where you and the boys will sleep," Madame Peré said.

Thérèse stood up and followed the older woman into the parlour.

"As you know, we have used this bed for anyone that is sick. We decided that since your time is near, you should have a comfortable bed to sleep in. Marguerite made it up for you this morning. The boys can sleep on pallets beside you, and Marie-Louise can sleep with my daughters."

"I appreciate your kindness to take my family in."

"Capitaine Peré and I are pleased to have you. We wanted to make sure you would be safe inside the walls when the fighting starts."

She choked up at the mention of her husband's name.

"My husband did not return when the soldiers retreated to the fortress. *Mon dieu*, I hope he is safe and not lying dead somewhere," she sobbed. She sniffed and dabbed at her nose with her handkerchief. "I have not told Anne and Madeleine the news yet. I am waiting to hear if there is further news of his whereabouts."

She touched the older woman's hand. "I will be here to support you and to help with the children in any way that I can."

"*Merci*. You are so kind, Thérèse. It must be so difficult for you to shoulder all the burdens without your husband. I will keep you and your children in my prayers."

# *Chapter Eighteen*

**Louisbourg, Île Royale, June 9–18, 1758**

Thérèse and the children settled into the Peré household as if they had always lived there. Thérèse helped Marguerite as much as she could. They made meals, looked after the children, cleaned and did laundry. The two women fell back into their old friendship, talking, laughing and enjoying their companionship. When Thérèse's back ached or her ankles were swollen, Marguerite insisted she lie down and rest. She figured her due date was around June 9th, and she hoped that the baby arrived before the battle between the British and French started in earnest. Madame Peré requested that food be prepared and put aside to have in case the women and children were evacuated to the casemates. Thérèse and Marguerite stacked essential items by the door that they could grab at a moment's notice. There was a chamber pot, candles, extra clothing, blankets and food prepared ahead.

Marie-Louise settled into her new surroundings and learned to feel her way around the house. Madeleine and Anne forgot about their initial discomfort and took her under their wings. The children all had chores, and Marie-Louise was happy to help in the kitchen. Philippe and Pierre were relieved to see their beloved chickens added to the Peré chicken coop. The boys were responsible for collecting the eggs and milking the goat, who made itself at home in their yard.

André visited the day after Thérèse and the children moved in. He had gone out to the fishing station and was horrified to see the destruction. He came at once to the Peré home and was relieved to find them all safe and sound. Marie-Louise was ecstatic to see her father and sat on his lap until he announced that he had to get back to his post. She clung to him and sobbed until Anne was able to coax her to playing with her doll. The little girl was eager to play with the older child and stopped crying.

A few days later, Thérèse was wondering when her little one would make its appearance into the world, when Lieutenant Duval dropped by with news. Madame Peré asked Marguerite to make coffee and he sat down at the kitchen table to have a cup.

"Do you have news of my husband?" Madame Peré asked.

"*Oui*, I do." He took a sip of his coffee before continuing. Madame Peré waited, an anxious look on her face.

"Your husband was one of the officers taken prisoner when the British landed."

Madame Peré smiled at the lieutenant. "*Merci Dieu,* he is alive. Do you know if he is well?"

Lieutenant Duval took several more sips of his coffee before answering her question. "Governor Drucourt sent a drummer out to the British camp with a letter to be delivered to Major General Amhurst, to inquire about the officers' wellbeing. Amhurst sent a reply back with the drummer to assure Governor Drucourt that the French officers were well and being cared for. He sent the Governor's wife a gift of two pineapples."

"Oh my, that was hospitable of the commander to send Madame Drucourt a gift," Madame Peré said.

"*Oui*, it was, and I heard that she wasn't to be outdone. She sent him a basket with fifty bottles of Burgundy wine."

Madame Peré smiled.

# Chapter Nineteen

**Louisbourg, Île Royale, June 19–20, 1758**

Thérèse was jolted awake. The house was dark, and she heard the roar of cannon fire in the distance. Something was happening. What was being bombarded? Were the British firing at the French soldiers? She reached up to touch her cross and prayed for God to help the French hold onto Louisbourg. The fighting did not sound close, but close enough, she thought. Something else was wrong, but what was it? Then she knew. A pain in her belly. It passed, but she remained awake, listening to the distant sound of cannons. Another pain came, and she gripped the sides of her bed. It was sharper than the previous one. She gritted her teeth so she wouldn't cry out and wake the household. When it passed, she relaxed. There was a lull in the shooting, but then it started up again. Another piercing pain seized her, and this time she groaned. She waited for it to pass before she eased herself out of bed and stumbled to the kitchen to wake Marguerite, who was sleeping on a pallet by the hearth. Marguerite jumped when she touched her.

"You scared me, Thérèse. I was having a bad dream that I was being chased by a red coat, and he had a musket pointed at my back."

"Well, I am not one of the red coats, but I think the baby is coming." Another pain came and she slumped down on the mattress.

Marguerite jumped up. "I will go and wake Madame Peré."

"I need the midwife. I think this one is coming fast."

Madame Peré appeared in the kitchen moments later.

"How far along do you think you are, Thérèse?"

"My pains are close together." Just then another one came, and she cried out. It was the sharpest one yet.

"Madame Peré, can you get the midwife?" she gasped when the pain subsided. She wanted Marguerite to stay with her.

"*Non*, it is best Marguerite fetch her. I am more experienced with these matters."

Marguerite turned as pale as a ghost in the dimly lit kitchen.

"Oh, please, do not make me go alone, Madame Peré. Let us go together. It is not safe for a woman to be out on her own after dark. I am terrified to go out there by myself. Do you not hear the gunfire?"

"Please, one of you stay with me," Thérèse cried. "What if the baby comes and I need help?"

"Marguerite, go at once and fetch the widow Droit. Take the lantern with you and hurry, I do not think we have much time."

Marguerite opened the door and a loud *boom* split the night air. She stepped back into the kitchen.

"Go, Marguerite, hurry!" Madame Peré scolded.

Marguerite fled the kitchen, slamming the door behind her.

"I will start getting things prepared for the widow Droit. Now, you just stay where you are. Do you want to lie down?"

She lay back to rest her head on the pillow and closed her eyes. She heard Madame Peré bustling about the kitchen, drawing the curtains to keep out peering eyes from women's business. She added logs to build up the fire, poured water into a kettle, and hung it on a hook over the fire to boil.

She thought Madame Peré looked out of place in the kitchen, usually occupied by her and Marguerite.

"The midwife will appreciate the hot water so she can clean things up. Oh, and I better get clean cloths." Madame Peré said.

"Could you get out the baby blanket I brought with me?" she asked between bouts of pain. The contractions were coming closer and closer together now.

"Where is it?"

"It is in that bundle beside my bed." Another pain seized her, and she screamed.

The door opened and Marguerite flew back in.

"That was quick," Madame Peré said, bustling into the kitchen with a pile of linens.

Marguerite was out of breath. "*Oui,* I saw a soldier walking up the street and I ran after him. When I got close, I saw it was Lieutenant Duval. I told him we needed the midwife at the Peré home, and he said he would go himself to get her. He will escort her here to make sure we do not need to send for the surgeon."

"*Non,* not the surgeon," Thérèse cried.

"Lieutenant Duval also said he would do anything to help Thérèse out. He told me she is such a charming lady." Marguerite winked at her friend. "I think the fellow is smitten with you, Thérèse."

She did not crack a smile at Marguerite's teasing. She was in her own little world of pain, and all she wanted at that moment was for the midwife to show up and get this baby out of her. Where was she? It seemed to be taking her a long time for her to get here. She hoped she was not tending to another birth.

Anne appeared at the kitchen door, dressed only in her chemise.

"Anne, what are you doing out of bed?" her mother exclaimed.

"I came to see what was wrong, *maman.* I could hear someone screaming and crying out. What is wrong with Thérèse? Is she sick?"

"*Non,* she is not sick, Anne, but this is no place for you to be right now. Now you go back upstairs and stay with the other children until we allow you to come down."

"But *maman,* I want to know what is wrong with Thérèse."

"You will find out soon enough. Now off with you, before I give you a good spank!" Madame Peré gave her daughter a gentle shove towards the stairs.

"When is the widow Droit going to get here?" Thérèse gripped the sides of the mattress when another pain pierced through her belly. She felt hot, and she was drenched in sweat.

"She will be here as soon as she can," Marguerite soothed, while she wiped her forehead with a cold cloth.

"I think the baby is coming," Thérèse said breathlessly.

She felt a hand grip hers and she looked up to see Madame Peré holding it.

"You are doing well, Thérèse. Just squeeze my hand tightly when you feel a pain."

Madame Peré began to recite a prayer.

"Oh mother of the holiest one of holies, who approached nearest to his divine perfection and so became mother to such a son, obtain for me by your grace . . . the favour to let me suffer with patience the pain which overwhelms me, and let me be delivered from this ill. Have compassion upon me. I cannot hold out without your help."

There was a knock at the door, and it opened, bringing the sounds of cannon fire closer.

"*Bonjour*, they are sure bombarding each other tonight," the widow Droit said, hanging her cloak over a kitchen chair. She took bottles filled with roots and medicine out of her basket and put them on the table. She then pulled out syringes and other instruments to have on hand.

"Where is the fighting?" Madame Peré asked

"Lieutenant Duval told me that the British on Lighthouse Point are firing at the island battery and the ships in the harbour."

Thérèse groaned loudly, interrupting the conversation.

The widow Droit hurried over to her.

"How are you doing, Thérèse?"

Before she could reply, the midwife lifted up her chemise to check on the baby's progress.

"The baby is coming, Thérèse. Now, I want you to push and push hard."

Marguerite got behind Thérèse and gripped her shoulders and Madame Peré took her hand. She pushed and pushed with all her might.

"*Très bien*, Thérèse. You are doing fine, but I need you to keep pushing. I see the baby's head. Can you give me one more big push?"

She mustered up all the strength she had left and gave a mighty push. She sighed with relief when she felt the infant slip into the midwife's hands. It was not crying. Thérèse panicked.

"My baby, is she all right?"

The widow Droit picked up her scissors, cut the umbilical cord and tied it off. There was still no crying from the infant, so she turned it over and gave it a slap on its bottom. The baby still did not breathe.

"My baby, what is wrong with my baby?" Thérèse wailed.

The widow Droit took a syringe and pried it into the infant's mouth. Then she took a tube, held it to her tiny mouth and blew into it. The rush of air caused a howl from the infant.

"You have a baby daughter, Thérèse. And, as it turns out, she has a good set of lungs." The midwife cleaned off the infant with the basin of water that Madame Peré had prepared for her and swaddled her in a blanket.

"Can I see her? Can I hold her?" Thérèse reached out for her infant daughter.

The widow Droit brought the baby over for her to see.

"You are so beautiful," she cooed to the tiny bundle.

"She is a fine baby. Now, before you hold her, let's get you cleaned up and change your chemise."

"My chemise that fastens in the front is in the bundle by my bed in the parlour. Could you get it for me, *s'il vous plait*?"

"I'll get it," Marguerite offered.

Thérèse was dressed and tucked into the bed in the parlour.

"Here is your baby daughter. She wants to be with her *maman*." The widow Droit placed the baby in her arms.

"*Ma petite*," she cooed to the infant. You are so beautiful, and you have your *papa*'s eyes." Tears trickled down her cheeks at the thought of Nicolas.

Marguerite bent over and had a look at the infant. "She is adorable, Thérèse."

Madame Peré stood behind Marguerite.

"Thérèse, the infant will need to be baptized as soon as possible. We must do it before the British start bombarding the town."

"Marguerite, would you and Gabriel be her Godparents?"

"*Oui*, Thérèse. We are pleased to be asked."

"What would you like to name her?"

Marguerite looked down at the sleeping infant. "I would like to name her Angélique. That was my mother's name."

"That is a beautiful name. It suits her."

"*Oui*," Marguerite agreed. She stepped back and Madame Peré took her turn at admiring the newborn.

The morning of Angélique's birth, Madame Peré made arrangements for the baby's baptism. True to his word, Lieutenant Duval called at the Peré home to check on the women.

"It was a terrible night of fighting. The British fired at the King's ships, and a cannon ball landed onboard the *Prudent*. The ship caught fire and the sailors managed to douse the flames before it destroyed the vessel.

Unfortunately, many of the sailors were injured. I heard that the King's ships are going to be moved as far away from Lighthouse Point as possible, to the end of the harbour, closest to the town."

Thérèse heard him speaking to Madame Peré from her bed in the parlour. She touched the cross that hung at the base of her neck.

Madame Peré asked Lieutenant Duval to fetch Gabriel from the forge, where he continued to repair ammunition. Père Aubré was to be summoned to baptize the newborn. Thérèse did not have a christening gown for the infant, and Madame Peré insisted she be wrapped in the white shawl that her children were baptized in. She looked angelic, tucked between the folds of the soft garment, and Thérèse kissed the top of her tiny head. Thérèse was not allowed to attend her child's baptism and could not enter the chapel until she was purified. She held the baby close for a moment. A feeling of foreboding overwhelmed her, and she was hesitant to give the infant up, for fear she would lose her too. What if a cannonball struck the chapel and her family was killed? What if… She felt anxious, as dreadful thoughts whirled through her mind. Tears filled her eyes and she dabbed at them with her sleeve.

"We must be on our way, Marguerite," Madame Peré ordered. "We do not want to be late for mass."

Thérèse took a deep breath and handed the baby over to Marguerite.

"We will have you back to your *maman* soon, little one. You will need to be fed," Marguerite cooed to the infant. "You will be fine, Thérèse. You try and get some sleep while the house is quiet. The widow Droit has offered to stay with you in case you need anything."

She continued to cry long after everyone left for mass. A deep sense of grief overwhelmed her and she wept for Nicolas. She wished he could have lived to see his first-born daughter. She could imagine the joy on his face when he held her for the first time.

The widow Droit appeared at her bedside and handed her a handkerchief to wipe her face.

"I brought you some tea to help you sleep. Could you sit up so you can drink it?" Thérèse sat up, and the midwife propped her pillow up so she could lean against it. She took a sip of the hot tea, and it felt soothing going down her throat.

"I know you must be missing Nicolas. There is not a day that goes by that I don't think of my own husband. But you are still young and must think of your children. You must stay strong for them. They need you. Especially now that we are at war with the British."

Thérèse nodded. Oh, she knew that she had to remain strong. There wasn't anything she wouldn't do to care for and protect them.

"Can I get you anything else?"

"Would you read my prayer book to me? My prayers bring me comfort and strength."

"*Mais oui*, Thérèse. Where is your prayer book?"

"It is on top of my trunk."

The widow Droit opened the book and began to read aloud. Thérèse lay back against the pillow and closed her eyes. She had attended many baptisms over the years and imagined her daughter's baptismal ceremony. Père Aubré would hold the infant in his arms and sprinkle her with holy water from the stone baptismal font, in the corner of the chapel. At the end of the ceremony, Père Aubré would sign his name in the parish registry. Marguerite and Gabriel couldn't read, so Père Aubré would sign the registry for them and they would put a cross beside their names. Madame Peré would sign her name as a witness. She smiled at the thought of her little daughter being named in heaven.

# *Chapter Twenty*

**Louisbourg, Île Royale, June 20–26, 1758**

The French cannons kept up a steady bombardment at the British, who were dug in at Lighthouse Point. The enemy fired back at the French naval ships in the harbour and the Island battery. Thérèse lay in bed, recuperating from childbirth, and the constant bombing distressed her. When would it ever end? What would happen to them? Would they make it out of this war alive? She prayed for the French soldiers, and for André Belliveau, who helped to man the cannons at Rochefort Point. She prayed he would not be taken from Marie-Louise. She didn't have a *maman,* and she didn't deserve to lose her *papa*, too. She prayed for Lieutenant Duval, who frequently visited the house to bring news of the battle. She cuddled her daughter tightly and watched her nurse. She thought of Nicolas and was thankful for his last gift to her. Angélique was so helpless and innocent. She worried that the infant would not thrive during the war, and she prayed for her other children to be safe and healthy.

After a few days of bedrest, she felt strong enough to get up and help with chores around the house. Her muscles were still sore and stiff, but it felt better to be up and doing things to help Marguerite and Madame Peré.

Everyone in the house enjoyed showering the baby with attention. Even Madame Peré wanted to a turn at fussing over her. André Belliveau visited the house as often as he could but was only permitted to stay for a few minutes. Marie-Louise was always delighted to see her *papa*, and she was excited to show him to the newest member of the house. When he arrived, she took his hand and led him over to the cradle to look at the sleeping infant.

"What's the baby's name?" André asked.

"Her name is Angélique Marie. She has my name, *papa*."

"*Oui*, she does, *ma petite*. Marie was your maman's name too."

André had tears in his eyes at the mention of his wife's name. He put his hands on the side of the cradle to stop Marie-Louise from rocking it too hard. Thérèse's heart went out to him. She understood what it was like to lose a loved one. She wanted to reach out and comfort him, but she knew it would not be proper. Instead, she gazed at him. He looked up and their eyes met. They gave each other a knowing look that meant that they knew what the other was going through. The connection was broken when André spoke to his daughter.

"We will let the baby sleep, and we will go and have a visit with the others." He took her hand and led her into the kitchen.

Every time André left to get back to his post, Marie-Louise was inconsolable.

Lieutenant Duval continued to visit the Peré home to check on the women. On one of these occasions, he had a frown on his face. He looked tired and had bags under his eyes. His clothes were disheveled and mud stained.

"What news do you bring?" Madame Peré asked.

"This siege is wearing everyone down," he said. "The British have knocked out the island battery."

"Oh, *mon dieu*," Madame Peré exclaimed.

Thérèse gasped and prayed for God to protect them.

"And now that the British have destroyed that defense, they are marching up to Green Hill to build batteries. It is the hill that overlooks the town."

"Oh *non*, I pray that isn't true," Madame Peré said.

"*Oui*, Madame, I wish I had better news, but I am afraid that the closer the British get to the fortifications, the more likely it is that they will launch an attack on the town." Lieutenant Duval turned to Thérèse.

"*Bonjour*, Madame Laserre." He smiled for the first time since entering the kitchen. "I have brought a bouquet of flowers to congratulate you on the birth of your daughter." She took the flowers from him and breathed in their fragrance.

"They are lovely. *Merci beaucoup*. What kind of flowers are they?"

"They are lady slippers."

"They are a lovely pink colour."

"*Oui*," Lieutenant Duval agreed.

Madeleine was holding the baby. Thérèse took the bundle from her and cradled Angélique in her arms so the officer could have a closer look at her. Philippe and Pierre stood beside her and looked up at their baby sister.

"How do you like having a sister, boys?" Lieutenant Duval asked.

"She cries too much," said Philippe.

"She dirties her diaper," Pierre said and wrinkled up his nose.

"Pierre, mind your manners in front of our guest," Thérèse scolded.

"Out of the mouths of babes," Lieutenant Duval chuckled. He bowed slightly to Thérèse and left the house.

# *Chapter Twenty-One*

**Louisbourg, Île Royale, June 26-July 1, 1758**

Thérèse thought she would never get used to the constant blast of cannons. The French guns continued to fire at the British work parties, digging batteries closer to the fortifications. It was impossible to ignore the battle raging outside the town, but she kept herself busy looking after the children and doing household chores.

Madame Peré became a frequent figure in the kitchen, helping Marguerite and Thérèse prepare food and other necessities if they had to evacuate their home and escape to the shelter of the casemates in the King's Bastion. She insisted that Thérèse take frequent breaks to rest. She would need all of her strength if there was an all out attack on the town.

A different side of Madame Peré was emerging. In the old days, when Thérèse lived in the household as a servant, the lady of the house was stern, and she was reserved in front of the servants and the children. Now, she was more relaxed and paid more attention to her children. She comforted them when they were frightened and gave them encouragement when it was needed. Thérèse recalled the days when she and Marguerite consoled them when they were distressed. Madame Peré was no longer as concerned about her social standing in the community. She was more focused on the well-being of friends and neighbours in the town, no matter their social status. Thérèse and Marguerite often helped her prepare baskets of food to share with families less fortunate then hers.

On one such occasion, she returned from delivering a basket of food to the nuns at the Congregation of Notre-Dame school for girls. Anne and Madeleine had not attended since the beginning of June, when the struggles between the English and French started. They begged to accompany their mother, but she refused to take them on account of the bombing. When she returned, Anne and Madeleine were anxious to find out how the sisters were managing.

"They were thankful for the basket of food I brought them. They have three orphaned girls in their care and rely on the donations of caring citizens to feed and clothe them. God has blessed us with such a caring community of people. I pray that he will take care of us and keep us safe during our troubles with the English."

"*Oui*," Thérèse and Marguerite agreed.

"The sisters wondered if you girls had any clothes you had outgrown. They could be altered for the orphaned children."

"*Oui, maman*, I can give them two of my dresses and a chemise," Anne offered.

"I can give them two of my dresses, and I could give them two of my dolls," Madeleine said.

"I have such good daughters. I am so proud of you. I wish you didn't have to live through this dreaded war." She gave them both a hug.

Madame Peré went on to tell them that she had met the governor's wife on her way home.

"Madame Drucourt told me that she was walking up to the ramparts to fire three cannon shots to boost the morale of the soldiers. I heard that she has walked up there every day since the fighting began and fires the cannon. She told me that she brings them food, too."

"What a courageous woman," said Marguerite.

"*Oui*, I admire Madame Drucourt. She is graceful and kind to everyone she meets," agreed Madame Peré.

"She was at Nicolas's funeral," Thérèse said.

"That was thoughtful of her to come," Marguerite said.

"I was pleased to see her in the congregation, and surprised, too, that someone of her status would come to a fisherman's funeral."

"*Oui*, she has her worries, too. She told me that Governor Drucourt is not well. His sciatica is bothering him. She said he is fraught with worry about Louisbourg's future, with the British Army so close to the town," Madame Peré said.

A few days later, Lieutenant Duval paid one of his frequent visits. As usual, he paid particular attention to Thérèse, even though the fighting was wearing him down. He looked haggard and worn but tipped his hat and gave her a special smile.

"I see your flowers are as beautiful as the day I brought them," he said.

"*Oui*, I am amazed that they are still blooming."

"You must be taking good care of them, Thérèse." He smiled at her once again.

"What news do you bring us today?" Madame Peré asked.

"Madame, the news is grim. Wolfe's companies of grenadiers have marched to the Dauphin Gate and the work parties are digging batteries in that area."

"Oh, *non*, may *le Bon Dieu* protect us from their madness," Madame Peré said.

Thérèse touched her cross. Marguerite nodded but didn't say a word. She had not been her usual bubbly self since Gabriel had joined the militia. Thérèse frequently heard her up in the night, and once she thought she heard her crying. Poor Marguerite, she would be lost if Gabriel was killed.

"The British are only seven or eight hundred yards from the gate. They are getting closer, and I beg you to take care of yourselves and the children. I think it would be best to pack up and head for the casemates in the King's Bastion. The soldiers have cleaned them out and have reinforced them with sand bags to protect them against bombs."

"We are fine here for now. I lived in Louisbourg during the last siege and I know what to expect. We have prepared food and made up bundles of blankets and pillows to take with us when the time comes," Madame Peré said.

"*Oui*, Madame, I am following your husband's orders. Before he was taken prisoner of war, he asked me to look out for his family, if anything happened to him. *Au revoir*," he said. He put on his tricorne hat and headed out the door.

# *Chapter Twenty-Two*

**Louisbourg, Île Royale, July 6, - 21, 1758**

"*Non*, get away from me," one of the children murmured.

It sounded like Madeleine's voice. Perhaps she was having a nightmare. The children were frightened by the bombing and didn't leave the adults' sides.

Thérèse sat in the armchair by the hearth, cuddling the baby. She kept her fastened in a sling worn over her shoulder. Marguerite and the children huddled on pallets on the floor. Madame Peré slept in the bed in the parlour. She heard the gentle rhythm of Marguerite snoring and one of the children thrashing about. It was probably Philippe, for he was a restless sleeper.

A pallet had been prepared for Thérèse to lie down on, but she found it impossible to sleep. The noise of the cannons distressed the baby and she cried, keeping the household awake. When she woke to be nursed, Thérèse didn't need to rise from her bed. She just opened her chemise and put the baby to her breast. She was content to sit up and rock Angélique until the motion of her rocking arms lulled them both to sleep.

The roar of cannons rumbled in the distance. The soldiers on the ramparts and the French ships in the harbour kept up a steady fire at the British work parties, who were digging in closer to the fortifications. But no matter how hard the French soldiers tried to prevent the enemy from launching an attack on the town, it seemed inevitable that bombs would soon be sailing over the walls.

Thérèse jumped when a mighty explosion rocked the house. Plaster rained down on her head. The windows shook, dishes rattled in cupboards, and she heard glass shattering. Was the bomb close or had it hit the house? The baby woke and let out a lusty wail. Marguerite screamed and all five children started to cry.

Thérèse was dazed at first. Had she been having a nightmare, or was this really happening?

"Everyone get up and dress at once," Madame Peré ordered, "and hurry. We must get to the shelters as fast as we can."

Everyone was frantic. They hastened to pull on clothes and gather up needed belongings to take with them. It was difficult to find anything in the darkness. Thérèse stumbled around to find her shawl, only to realize she was wearing it. She helped Marie-Louise into her shoes and made sure that Philippe and Pierre had their warmest clothes on. Meanwhile, bombs continued to whistle overhead. The children were frightened and clung to the adults who were anxious to get them to the safety of the casemates. Madame Peré and her daughters were the last ones to leave the house. Thérèse walked ahead of them and when she looked back, Madame Peré had stopped to look back at her home.

"Come on, Madame Peré, hurry! It is too dangerous to stop."

Her voice was drowned out by a bomb that sailed past them and exploded on the roof of a neighbour's home. She kept moving through the dark streets for fear of being killed. The only light came from burning buildings. She followed Marguerite, who carried Marie-Louise while Pierre and Philippe clung to her skirts. The walk to the shelters seemed endless. Her heart raced, and her body shook from fright. The air was thick with smoke, and she heard the snap and crackle of burning buildings. Children cried and women screamed with every bomb that crashed down around them. Finally, they reached the casemates. Each shelter had a door and one small window. She followed Marguerite into the dark interior and stepped down onto a dirt floor. The chamber was damp and smelled musty. The room was pitch black until one of the women lit a lantern. When her eyes adjusted to the dim light, Thérèse was able to make out the room's stone walls and curved ceiling. Debris from fallen masonry littered the floor. Where were they going to sit? Where were they going to spread out the blankets they brought? Hopefully not on the dirty floor. Sandbags were stacked against the walls. Madame Peré, Marguerite, and two other women re-arranged them to make seats.

"Here, Thérèse," Marguerite patted one of the sandbags. "Why don't you put the baby down for a little while, so you can have a rest."

She rocked Angélique gently in her arms. It soothed her and she stopped crying.

"I'm afraid she will start to cry again if I put her down. I don't want to disturb everyone."

"Nonsense, Thérèse, you won't be able to hold her the whole time we are down here," Marguerite said as she spread out a blanket so Thérèse could put the baby down. She took a seat beside her friend and tucked the blanket up around her. Marie-Louise cuddled up beside her, and the boys sat beside the little girl. Anne and Madeleine sat between Marguerite and their mother. The girls complained that they were cold, so Marguerite wrapped them in blankets.

The bombs had not let up since they entered the shelter. The ground vibrated beneath their feet and the walls shook with every explosion.

"I'm scared," Marie-Louise cried. Thérèse put her arm around the child and realized that she was shaking, so she wrapped a blanket around her.

"I know. We're all scared. But we must pray for your *papa*'s safety and for all the other soldiers who are out there protecting Louisbourg. Would you pray with me?"

"*Oui*, the little girl agreed. Thérèse reached into her pocket and brought out her rosary beads. She made the sign of the cross and other women did the same. She began to say the "Apostles Creed" aloud.

"I believe in God, the Father Almighty, Creator of Heaven and earth; and in Jesus Christ . . ."

Some of the women recited it with her and they continued to say the "Our Father Prayer."

"Our Father, Who art in heaven, hallowed be Thy name. . ."

Thérèse moved her fingers along her rosary until she reached three small beads.

"Hail Mary, full of grace. The Lord is with thee."

When she looked up, some of the women continued to pray out loud and others sat in silence. The children slept beside her, oblivious to the noisy cannons above their heads. When Thérèse looked around the dimly lit interior, she saw that some of the women were also sleeping. Marguerite and

Madame Peré continued to pray out loud, and it wasn't long before the sound of their voices lulled her to sleep.

Thérèse woke to cannon blasts and her crying infant. She picked her up and tucked her beneath her cloak to nurse her. She looked up at the window above her and saw that it was daylight. The fighting had gone on all night, and they were still pounding at each other. How long would this go on? Would there be anything left of the town? Would Madame Peré's house still be standing when this was all over?

The women and children began to stir.

"*Maman*, I'm thirsty," Pierre wined.

Marguerite rose from her seat and gave them each a dipper full of water. Madame Peré dug into the food supply and handed out pieces of biscuit and cheese.

Thérèse looked up when the door to the shelter opened and Lieutenant Duval entered. She stood to greet him, baby Angélique tucked under her arm, and Madame Peré, right behind her.

"*Bonjour, Mesdames*. I can only stay a few minutes, but I came to make sure you were all right."

"*Oui,* Lieutenant Duval. We are doing as well as can be expected, under the circumstances. Do you have news for us?" Madame Peré asked.

He had a grim expression on his face. "The news is not good. The hospital was hit last night."

Madame Peré gasped. "Was anyone hurt or killed?"

He nodded. "A surgeon was killed."

"May God rest his soul," Thérèse whispered as she touched her cross.

He sighed before continuing. "And two of the Brothers of Charity were injured in the explosion."

"Madame Peré let out a loud sigh.

"The fighting has temporarily stopped. Governor Drucourt asked for a truce and has sent a note to the British commanders asking them for a safe place for the wounded since there is no room within the town to house them."

"Ah, that is why it is quiet." Madame Peré said.

"*Oui*, Madame. I opened the Dauphin Gate to let the French officer out with a white flag to signal a truce. When the firing ceased, I stepped outside the walls to see what was happening.

"*Bonjour, mesdames. Comment allez-vous?*" he asked Thérèse and Marguerite.

"*Nous allons bien,*" Thérèse said. "Do you know what happened to Gabriel Pineau or André Belliveau?"

"*Non*, Madame, I have not seen them."

Marguerite looked worried, and Thérèse put her arm around her.

"*Comment vas-tu?*" Madame Peré asked the lieutenant.

"*Je vais bien. Merci beaucoup*. I was surveying the damage to the fortifications when I witnessed an interesting scene. A British officer and his wife were out for a walk and they approached Sieur Boisvert. He can speak English and exchanged pleasantries with them. The officer introduced his wife to him and during their conversation, they discovered that they may be distant cousins. The lady said that she had noticed the gardens outside the walls and wondered if she might pick vegetables for a salad. Of course, my friend being the gentleman that he is with the ladies, gave her permission to do so. I watched the couple stroll away in the direction of Madame Laserre's garden."

Thérèse's ears perked up and she bristled at the thought of the British lady raiding her garden. How dare the French officer allow this stranger to pick her lettuce? She had spent hours bent over planting those seeds! Now the fruits of her labour were going into the mouths of the enemy. The rumble of cannon fire in the distance made her flinch, and she went back into the shelter.

# Chapter Twenty-Three

### Louisbourg, Île Royale, July 9, 1758

Minutes passed. Hours passed. The women and children huddled in their tomb-like chamber, no one daring to venture outside. The children grew restless, and the adults entertained them by singing and telling them stories. Thérèse's head ached from the constant roar of the cannons overhead. She was filthy after not washing her hands and face for hours. Her skirt was covered in food stains, and her chemise bore spots where the baby had spit up on her. The enclosure reeked of body odor and sweat. The chamber pot in the corner smelled foul, making her nauseous. She found it difficult to swallow but forced herself to eat to keep her breast milk from drying up.

She stood up to stretch her legs and climbed the stairs to the entrance. She opened the door a crack and, to her surprise, there was silence. Not one cannon blasted. What was happening? Was it over? She hoped so. A soldier stood a few feet away, a pipe clenched between his teeth. She stepped out of the shelter and walked over to speak with him. The sun was bright after so many hours of semi-darkness. There was a strong wind blowing and the smell of smoke hung in the air.

"*Bonjour, soldat.* Can you tell me what is going on? Why is it so quiet?"

The soldier took his pipe out of his mouth. "The French have asked the British for a ceasefire to bury the dead."

She gripped her cross. "The dead? What happened? Who was killed?"

"There was a sortie last night outside the Queen's Gate. A contingent of our soldiers surprised the British. It was a bloody battle, Madame. There were fifty or sixty men killed at the hands of British bayonets, and one officer was wounded."

Her heart raced. "Do you know if André Belliveau, Lieutenant Duval or Gabriel Pineau were among those soldiers?"

"*Non*, Madame, I am sorry. I do not know those men. You and the other women might as well come out into the sunshine."

"*Oui, merci, soldat.*"

She hurried back into the shelter to give the women the sad news and to let them know that it was safe to leave the casemates during the ceasefire.

The lull in the bombing was a welcome respite. The women and children walked through the rubble strewn streets littered with pieces of mortar and debris from buildings that had been hit. They walked around craters, gouged out from cannon fire, where cobblestones had once been. Many houses were partially standing or had been reduced to ashes. They reached the Peré home to find that it had not been destroyed, and Madame Peré sighed with relief.

Marguerite retrieved a bucket of water from the well and poured it into a basin so they could wash their hands and faces. Thérèse helped the children clean themselves before taking her turn. The scent of lavender from the soap smelled heavenly after living in cramped, foul smelling quarters. She took her time washing and toweling herself dry. She put on a clean chemise and skirt. The boys refused to change their clothes, so she resigned herself to dropping the matter. She didn't want to make a scene in front of the other women. She helped Marie-Louise into clean clothes and all the while, the little girl asked for her *papa*.

"Where is he? I want to see him," she pleaded.

Thérèse felt tears sting her eyes. She was afraid of what may have happened to André Belliveau but didn't want to upset Marie-Louise unnecessarily. She hugged the little girl and held her close.

"I don't know where your *papa* is, little one, but I can assure you that he loves you very much."

Food was gathered up and other necessities were added to their stash for their confinement before they headed back outside to enjoy the much-needed sunshine. The children chased each other around the yard while the women picked vegetables and herbs out of the garden.

"I wish I could pick a fresh basket of wild strawberries. They must be ready to pick by now," Marguerite mused.

"*Oui*, you are making my mouth water. Wouldn't a strawberry pie be tasty?" Thérèse said.

"*Oui*," Madame Peré agreed. "I can imagine that the Brits are feasting on them this year."

"Look who is coming up the street," Marguerite announced. "It is André Belliveau!"

"*Papa*, *papa*!" The little girl ran to her father's waiting arms.

"I have missed you, *ma petitte,* and I thought about you all the time." He picked her up and held her close.

Thérèse was glad that Marie-Louise could not see the state of her *papa*'s clothes. His coat was covered in blood stains and mud. She shuddered. What atrocities had he witnessed? He put the little girl down.

"You run along and play with the other children. *Papa* needs to talk to the ladies."

"Oh, *papa*, I want to stay with you!" The little girl cried.

"Come now, Marie-Louise, *papa* only has a few minutes."

Anne took Marie-Louise by the hand and led her away from the adults. Thérèse had a sinking feeling in the pit of her stomach that André was bringing bad news. He turned to Marguerite.

"I am so sorry, Marguerite, to have to tell you,"

Marguerite turned pale. "Is it Gabriel? Is he hurt? Where is he?"

Thérèse put an arm around her friend.

"Take it easy, Marguerite. Just listen to what André has to tell us."

"Gabriel was injured last night during the sortie. I was fighting alongside him when I saw him go down. A British musket ball hit him in the leg. He was bleeding heavily and in a lot of pain. I carried him back to the town where he could get medical attention."

"Where is he now? I want to see him. Can you take me to him?"

"Gabriel is at the Hopital Roi and is being well cared for by the Frères de La Charité."

"I want to see him!" Marguerite cried. "I will go to the Hopital Roi right now"

"*Non*, I suggest you head back to the shelter with the other women. It is not safe for you to walk alone. I assure you that he is well cared for. You must keep yourself out of harm's way."

A cannon rumbled in the distance reminding them that they were not at peace yet.

# *Chapter Twenty-Four*

**Louisbourg, Île Royale, mid-July 1758**

Spirits were low in the shelters. Many of the women grieved for loved ones who had died in battle, and others worried about husbands or sons who were wounded. Marguerite was frantic for news of Gabriel. Thérèse and Madame Peré tried to assure her that he was well cared for by the brothers at the King's Hospital. Père Aubré frequently stopped by to pray with the women and often brought news about soldiers who were wounded and assured Marguerite that Gabriel's injury was healing nicely. It seemed that they all needed prayers. What was to become of them? How would this conflict be resolved? Was there ever going to be an end to the fighting? The fortifications were crumbling and there were breaches in walls. Nevertheless, the siege dragged on. The British kept on battering the town, and the French kept up a steady fight.

During one of his visits Père Aubré spoke with Thérèse.

"Shortly after your marriage to Monsieur Laserre, he came to see me. He gave me a letter and asked if I could keep it in my possession. In the event of his death, he asked that I give it to you."

Her eyes filled with tears at the mention of Nicolas. Why would he write her a letter and give it to the priest?

Père Aubré handed it to her. "Would you like me to be with you when you read it?"

"*Non merci,* I would like to read it privately."

"Very well, Madame. I will let you read it when you are ready. May I pray with you and your children?"

"*Oui,* that would be kind of you."

There was never a good time to read the letter, so it remained in her pocket until she had a private moment. The children were restless and cranky. Tempers flared between the older children, often ending in tears. She scolded when necessary and soothed when it was needed. She knew how difficult it was for all of them to be confined to such a small space with no sign of ever getting out.

The crowded conditions of the women and children were bad enough, but they got worse. Marie-Louise was the first child in their shelter to complain of feeling cold and having a sore throat. All Thérèse could do was bundle her in blankets. She would have made her herbal tea to soothe her throat, but she did not have a fire to boil water. The little girl whimpered, and the only thing Thérèse could do was to hold her. Madame Peré had left their shelter to check on families in neighbouring casemates. When she returned, the widow Droit was with her. Thérèse had her take a look at Marie-Louise.

"What is wrong with her? She can't seem to stop shivering, and she is complaining of a sore throat."

The widow Droit bent over and touched the child's forehead. She has a fever. I am afraid that she has *la grippe*. I have been tending to families in other shelters who are complaining of similar symptoms."

"I wish I could boil water for hot tea," Thérèse said.

"I will build a fire just outside the shelters," offered the widow Droit.

"That is too dangerous," Madame Peré said. "There is too much cannon fire at this time."

"Don't you worry. I will build it as close to the wall as possible. I am afraid that many people will be needing cures, given the conditions that we are living in."

"*Oui*, I will help and will fetch water for you."

"*Merci*, Madame Peré.

Thérèse kept Marie-Louise comfortable while the preparations were underway. She held her on her lap and sang quietly, in the hope of putting her to sleep. The little girl did not sleep and continued to fuss.

"I want my *papa*," she cried in a croaky voice.

"He'll be here soon."

Thérèse wondered where André was and prayed that he was safe. She looked up when she heard the door to the shelter open. Madame Peré entered, carrying a mug.

"The widow Droit said to give this to Marie-Louise to soothe her throat."

"What is it?" Thérèse asked.

"It is sage tea."

"I will give her some, but I don't know if it will taste good."

She sat Marie-Louise up, took the mug from Madame Peré, and put it to the child's lips. Marie-Louise took a sip and screwed up her face.

"I know it doesn't taste good, but you must drink some so it can help make your throat better."

Marie-Louise nodded and drank some more. When she had enough, she crawled back onto Thérèse's lap and was asleep in minutes. She had just dosed off when she felt a tap on her shoulder. Marie-Louise

"*Maman,*" Pierre whined, "My throat hurts."

"Oh, no, not you too."

She felt her son's forehead. He felt hot. "Are you cold?"

"*Oui, maman.*"

"This will keep you warm." Madame Peré picked up a quilt and wrapped it around him. "Why don't you come here and sit beside Anne and Madeleine. They are complaining of having chills, too." To Thérèse, she said, "How is the baby?"

She had Angélique snuggled against her breast. "She has an appetite, but she feels warmer than normal. Do you think she has a fever?"

Madame Peré touched the baby's forehead. "*Oui,* she feels warm."

Thérèse unwrapped Angélique's blanket and when she touched her skin she began to wail. Marguerite, who had been tucking Pierre's quilt around him, came to examine the baby. She reached out and touched the baby's cheeks.

"*Oui,* she is feverish. I will go and fetch more water and will gather up cloths so we can bathe her. That will help to cool her down."

Madame Peré put on her cloak. "I will accompany you, Marguerite. I do not want you to go alone."

The women prepared to leave the shelter, grabbing buckets for water.

"Be safe," Thérèse called out when they left. She reached for the cross that hung around her neck. "Please, God, protect us all and please don't take our children from us."

Phillipe was the next child in the shelter to come down with *La grippe.* Thérèse bundled him up and tucked him in beside the others. She gave them sips of water and soothed when needed. The bombing did not let up, and the children frequently cried out that they were scared. She gave them all hugs and re-assured them that they were safe in the shelter. She nervously waited for Madame Peré and Marguerite to return. When they were not back within a half-hour, she became worried. What could be taking them so long? Could something have happened to them? Her worries were forgotten when Anne and Madeleine complained of a sore throat. She put on her shawl, grabbed mugs, and headed outside to get hot water for sage tea. When she reached the fire she found Madame Peré and Marguerite talking to the widow Droit.

"I am glad to see you two are back safely. I was worried. You were gone such a long time."

"*Je suis désolée*, Thérèse," Madame Peré said. "The widow Droit has just given us some bad news."

Thérèse clutched her little wooden cross. "What is it?"

Marguerite came and put her arms around her. "*La grippe* has taken two children. They died this morning."

"They could not fight it any longer," the widow Droit said.

"Oh *non*. May they rest in peace and may they be with the Lord," Thérèse said.

"Père Aubré is praying with the families now," Madame Peré said.

Thérèse returned to the shelter with a heavy heart. How could such innocent little lives be taken so quickly? She prayed for her own children, for Madame Peré's daughters, and for all the other colonists.

She gave mugs of sage tea to the children. Pierre took a sip of his and refused to drink the rest. She wished there was syrup to put in it to help get it down. She tried to get him to drink several more times, but each time he pushed the mug away.

The morning turned into afternoon, and Marie-Louise took a turn for the worse. She had a high fever and became delirious, thrashing about and crying out. While the others rested, Thérèse sat by the little girl and applied cold cloths all over her body in an attempt to cool her down. She wondered where her *papa* was and wished he would drop by to see her. He needed to know that she was ill, but she had no way of finding him. She was afraid the fever might not break and the little girl would succumb. She was putting a wet cloth on her forehead when a series of explosions shook the earth. She jumped with fright, causing the pot of water to tip. Marie-Louise's eyes fluttered open. Thérèse hoped that she was coming out of her delirium, but the child's eyes closed and she fell back into a deep sleep.

"What was that? What is happening?" Madame Peré asked.

"I don't know," Thérèse said. "It didn't sound like cannon fire. It sounded more like something exploded."

"*Oui*, it did," Marguerite agreed.

Thérèse thought Marguerite had been sleeping, but the commotion must have woken her. She looked tired and had complained of a headache. The widow Droit had made a tea with meadowsweet to help relieve the pain.

"How are you feeling, Marguerite? Did the tea help?"

"*Oui*, it did help, and I feel better now that I had a rest."

The children stirred, and the adults got up to tend to their needs.

Later that night, when the children had settled down, Thérèse felt exhausted. She too, had a headache and used some of the widow Droit's meadowsweet to make herself a tea. She leaned back and finally dosed off. She woke with a start when there was a knock at the door. Madame Peré climbed the stairs to let the visitor in. She was glad to hear André's voice. She checked on Marie-Louise and was relieved to find that her fever had broken. The little girl's eyes were open, and she smiled when she heard her *papa* at her side.

"*Papa*, you came at last."

"*Oui, ma petite*." He scooped Marie-Louise up into his arms.

"She has been a sick little girl," Thérèse said.

"I am so glad you are feeling better now. I wish I could have been with you."

Marie-Louise clung to him and would not let go when he tried to put her back under the quilt. "Don't go, *papa*. Please stay with me."

"I am not going yet. I want to talk to the adults but I will come back to see you. You keep warm and get feeling better." He tucked the quilt around her.

He stood up to speak to the women, and he had a frown on his face. His eyes were dull, and he looked thinner than he did before the siege. Food had become scarce, and no one was eating well.

"Do you have news of the siege?" Thérèse asked.

"*Oui*, three French ships in the harbour were lost today."

Madame Peré gasped. "*Oh non.*"

André nodded. "*L'Entreprenant* was hit by a British mortar shell. It hit the poop deck."

He was interrupted by giggles from the children. "The poop deck," they laughed.

"Be quiet," Madame Peré scolded. "We want to hear what happened."

"The bomb hit powder cartridges and they exploded. The ship caught fire, and the wind quickly spread flames to *Le Célèbre* and *Le Capricieux.* The fires could not be controlled. *L'Entreprenant* exploded, and the other two ships were destroyed."

Thérèse was stunned. No one spoke.

Finally, she said, "Those were the explosions we heard this afternoon."

"*Oui*, it happened around two o'clock, André confirmed.

Madame Peré was as pale as a ghost in the dark interior. "*Mon Dieu!* What a loss it is for the French."

# *Chapter Twenty-Five*

**Louisbourg, Île Royale, mid-July 1758**

Could news of the siege get any worse? Thérèse often reached for the rosary in her pocket. She thanked God for the children's recovery from la grippe, for the safety of her family and for all the soldiers fighting for their colony. The French were being battered, but their guns kept up a steady fire at the British, who were now just outside the walls. Every cannon blast increased her need to worry. The other women around her shared the same concerns, with their pinched looks and pale faces. What would happen to her family? How would they survive? Their home and livelihood went up in smoke and she had no money to start over. What would happen if the British took Île Royale? Would the colonists be deported back to France? It happened to them in the past, so it could happen again. That would mean a long ocean crossing with three children in tow. She remembered her ocean voyage, nine years earlier, and shuddered. It had been a rough one, with many passengers becoming ill. A number of older people and young infants did not make it to Louisbourg. Her eyes filled with tears at the thought of losing her children, and she dabbed at them with her handkerchief. What would happen once they arrived in France? She knew her family would welcome her and her children with open arms, but how would they get to La Rochelle with no money? She didn't even know if her family was still living there or if they were still alive. The blockade had made letters scarce, and she had not heard from her father or brother for months.

"I smell smoke," Marie-Louise said in her soft voice.

"Pardon, Marie-Louise. What was that you said?" Thérèse asked.

"I smell smoke," she said again.

"It is from the bonfire outside," Marguerite assured her.

The little girl did have a good sense of smell, but Thérèse caught a whiff of it too and decided to check the bonfire. It was early morning, around seven o'clock, when she emerged from the shelter. The fire had died down over night and there were only a few small embers burning. There was no other sign of smoke, so she went back inside.

"Everything seems fine," she reported and settled back down to nurse the baby. Everyone still seemed sleepy and they all continued to huddle together in silence. The only sounds for the next hour were the roar of cannons above them.

"Fire," a male voice shouted from outside. Thérèse was instantly alert.

"The barracks are on fire," someone yelled.

"Evacuate the casemates at once," the voice came again.

The acrid smell of smoke filled the darkened chamber.

"We must get out," Madame Peré shouted, "and hurry!"

Everyone was on their feet. Thérèse snatched up the baby and hurried to catch up with the boys who had raced ahead of her.

"Stay with *maman*. Hang onto my skirts so you don't get lost."

Neither child heard her command over the screams and cries of others around them. There was utter confusion outside the casemates. The smoke was so dense she couldn't see where she was going. Where were the boys? They had been right in front of her.

"Philippe! Pierre!" she yelled above the din.

Neither child came when she called.

"Oh, why didn't you stay with me when I asked you to?" she said out loud between sobs.

She kept moving and called out the boy's names. She tucked the baby inside her shawl so she wouldn't breathe in the acrid smell. The smoke tickled her throat and she coughed. Where were her sons? Where were the other women and children? Marguerite, who had been carrying Marie-Louise, was right behind her when they vacated the shelter. Madame Peré and her daughters were the last ones to leave. Where had they gone? Wouldn't one of them hear her calling for the boys? Women and children ran in all directions, trying to get away from the burning building. Soldiers rushed by with buckets of water to extinguish the fire. Injured men were carried out of the casemates on stretchers. The bombing had not let up, and no one knew where to put the injured officers. The ground beneath her rumbled and shook from the explosions. When a bomb erupted behind her, she and the baby were forced to the ground and the world went black.

# *Chapter Twenty-Six*

**Louisbourg, Île Royale, July 22, 1758**

Thérèse opened her eyes. She lay on the ground with the baby tucked beneath her. She prayed that the blanket and shawl had protected her from the fall. Where were the boys? She remembered calling their names before she fell. Women and children screamed and cried for help but none of them came from Philippe or Pierre. Men called out for more water to douse the blaze. Cannon blasts continued to shatter the world around her. This was a horrid nightmare, she thought, except that it was really happening. She coughed and spit dust out of her mouth. A hand touched her arm.

"*Mon Dieu*, Madame Laserre! I got such a fright when I saw you on the ground." Lieutenant Duval stood over her.

"My children. Where are they?" she cried.

"I have not seen your children."

"The boys. I can't find Philippe and Pierre," she said in a hoarse voice.

"I will look for the boys, but first I will escort you to Madame Peré's home to see if they have turned up there. Can you stand up?"

"*Oui*." She took the hand he offered and got to her feet. She felt weak and her legs trembled. Her head throbbed and it felt like her entire body was bruised. She put one foot in front of the other and made herself move. She had to. She had to find her little boys.

"Take my arm, Madame, to support yourself and I will get you out of harm's way."

"I just want to find my children,' she cried.

She was still too stunned to walk by herself, so with her crying infant in one arm, she linked the other one through his.

"Will Madame Peré know to go to her home?"

"*Oui*, I met Madame Peré and her daughters on my way to the King's Bastion. I escorted them to the house before coming back to look for you. They lost track of you in the thick smoke and were worried about you and the boys."

"Was Marguerite Pineau with them?"

"*Non*, but Madame Peré was worried about her too, and she said Marguerite was carrying a little girl."

She silently prayed for their safety.

The lieutenant led her out of the Kings Bastion and away from the smoke and flames. She hadn't been beyond the confines of the casemate for days, and when they reached the street, she was shocked by the destruction. There were empty spaces where buildings had once stood. Some houses were damaged and falling into ruins. Rubble and debris littered the ground, and she stepped around craters that had been gouged out from mortar explosions.

The Peré home stood untouched, but she noticed that the last few weeks of bombardment had taken its toll on the structure. Shutters hung loose, and window glass lay strewn about the yard. A piece of mortar shot had embedded itself right in the centre of the door.

"Not one building in town has been left unscathed," Lieutenant Duval said. He knocked on the door.

Madame Peré and Marguerite greeted the Lieutenant and rushed to embrace Thérèse.

"I am so glad to see you," Madame Peré said.

"I was so worried about you," Marguerite said. When I realized you weren't in front of me anymore, I just kept walking and hoped we would all end up back here. When I arrived and you and the boys weren't here, I wanted to go out and look for you, but Madame Peré would not hear of it."

Thérèse looked around the room, hoping to see Philippe and Pierre, but they were not there. Her heart sank.

"My little boys," she wailed, "they were right in front of me! And then they were gone. I must go out and look for them. They will be so frightened out there."

"*Non*, Madame, I will go and look for them. You have had a fall and are not well enough to be out looking for them," Lieutenant Duval insisted.

Tears filled her eyes, and she couldn't control them. Marguerite put an arm around her and led her to an armchair.

"I will be back as soon as I can," Lieutenant Duval said and hurried out the door.

Now, all Thérèse could do was wait and pray.

# *Chapter Twenty-Seven*

**Louisbourg, Île Royale, July 22-23, 1758**

The waiting stretched on, and there was no sign of the boys. The women and children huddled together in blankets, beneath a makeshift shelter—a table covered with sheets and quilts to protect them from the possibility of falling debris. No one spoke. They hadn't eaten anything yet, but no one was hungry. The events of the day had robbed them of appetites.

Lieutenant Duval came back later in the afternoon with the grim news. He was unable to find Philippe and Pierre. He had looked everywhere and asked anyone if they had seen two little boys wandering by themselves. No one had seen them.

Thérèse was frantic. Where could they have gone? If no one had seen them, then they must have been killed. She held onto her rosary but was unable to pray. Tears rolled down her face, and she didn't have the energy to wipe them away. The lieutenant's report about the fire barely registered.

"The fire in the King's Bastion Barracks had finally been put out. The soldiers' quarters and the chapel were destroyed, but the governor's apartments remained untouched." Lieutenant Duval shook his head.

"It's a sad situation. The fortifications are crumbling, embrasures are destroyed and gun batteries all around the town have been knocked out."

Thérèse was not worried about the town's destruction. All she wanted was to see her little boys alive and well.

Madame Peré thanked the lieutenant for dropping by to tell them the news. He left to report for duty, and the women and children settled back down to wait.

The waiting seemed endless, and when Thérèse thought she could stand it no longer, an idea came to her. She thought she might know where the boys were hiding. She didn't know if Lieutenant Duval had searched that spot, but there was only one way to find out. She whispered to Marguerite that she would be back shortly and crept quietly out of the makeshift shelter. She bolted out the door and ran as fast as she could, narrowly missing a large crater in the cobblestones. She kicked rubble out of her path and dodged cannon shots. She ran up the hill toward the King's Bastion, and then she ran right into a soldier. She cried out when he stuck out his arm to stop her from running him over. When she looked up, she saw Soldat Bouchet glaring at her.

"Madame Laserre, why are you running and why are you out here?"

She was out of breath. "My little boys. Philippe and Pierre. They are missing. I think I might know where they are. They loved to look over the fence at the Governor's horses, and I want to go and see if that is where they have gone."

"Madame, you cannot go there. It is too dangerous. I won't allow you to go. I will go and check the stables for you."

"*Non*, I am going to see for myself, and a team of wild horses couldn't stop me, so let me go!"

"Madame, allow me to escort you there, then."

She nodded, and they hurried up the hill. When they reached the stables, the boys were nowhere in sight, and neither were the horses.

"I'll check inside the stable, in case they are hiding in there," Soldat Bouchet said.

She followed him to the door. It took her a moment to adjust her eyes to the dim interior. The soldier had entered, and she heard him talking. When he emerged from behind the Governor's buggy, he was not alone.

"I have found two brave young men," he said.

"Philippe and Pierre!" She cried and ran to them with open arms. She hugged them tightly and didn't let go until they squirmed to get free. Her heart was filled with gladness at the sight of them. She was so happy to see them that she couldn't speak for the lump in her throat, and tears of joy rolled down her cheeks.

Finally, she found her voice. "I have been so worried about you both."

"I found two little frightened boys huddled in a pile of straw. They must have kept running straight instead of turning into the central passageway, but they found a safe place to hide."

"Is that what happened, boys?"

"*Oui, maman.* We got lost and we couldn't find you anywhere," Philippe explained.

"*Oh, mes petits,*" she hugged both of her children again. "I called your names many times, but you could not hear me over the loud guns."

She finally looked up to see Soldat Bouchet looking at her. His eyes glowed with pride. "It was my pleasure to help you find your sons, Madame Laserre."

"*Merci beaucoup.* I was so worried something had happened to them."

"I am hoping that now you will forgive me for my wrongdoings. I believe it won't be long before the French are forced to surrender, and when that happens, I would hate for you to be forced into marrying a British soldier. Marry me, Madame Laserre, so I can protect you and your children."

She gasped. What was she to say to this man who had deceived her and was now asking for her hand in marriage? The thought of marrying him was unthinkable. Besides, the French were still pursuing their attackers.

"I will always be grateful to you for helping to rescue my children, and I can find it in my heart to forgive you."

The soldier gave her a big smile. "*Oui,* Madame."

"But I cannot find it within myself to enter into marriage with you."

Soldat Bouchet's face fell with those words. "*Au revoir,*" he said, turned his back and left her and the children in front of the Peré home.

# *Chapter Twenty-Eight*

**Louisbourg, Île Royale, July 24, 1758**

The hours of sitting huddled together in their makeshift shelter seemed endless. Thérèse wished the fighting would end so life could get back to normal again. But would it? Madame Peré seemed to think that the French would eventually have to surrender. Thérèse thought the conflict had gone on far too long, and she felt sad to think that it was possible that the colonists would be deported to France. But it might give her an opportunity to see her family again. She hadn't seen any of them since she left La Rochelle, nine years ago. So much had happened in such a short time. She hated to think of leaving her husband behind in a cold grave, with no one to tend it with love and care. Her thoughts were interrupted by a tug on her sleeve.

"Thérèse, we have a visitor." Marguerite nudged her in the side. "You were deep in thought. Did you not hear me talking to you?"

Thérèse shook her head. She was glad for the interruption. Her thoughts were making her feel too sad.

"Come in, Monsieur Belliveau and have a seat," Madame Peré said. Thérèse crawled out from beneath the table. She felt silly crawling out of her hiding place. It felt like she was back in her childhood, playing make-believe. When André saw her, he gave her a weary smile. He put out his hand and helped her to her feet. Marie-Louise followed her and hurried to give her *papa* a hug. He scooped her up and sat her on his lap.

"This is a pleasant surprise to see you," Thérèse said.

"*Oui*, I am glad to have a break, but I am only allowed to take a few minutes."

André looked exhausted. He was pale and had dark shadows under his eyes. His hair, usually tied back, hung loose and was stringy. His clothes were filthy and hung on his too-skinny frame. He was probably living on meager rations these days.

"Is there anything we can do for you?" Thérèse asked him. "Can we get you something to eat? Something to drink?"

"I would like something to eat, and a drink would be nice to go with it."

She left the visitors to make up a plate of biscuits topped with currant jam and poured him a cup of angelica tea.

"What news do you bring from the outside world?" Madame Peré asked.

"There is no good news, Madame Peré. The town is in a sad state. There was another bad fire last night. The barracks in the Queen's Bastion burned down, and two houses nearby were also destroyed. I don't know why the Brits are destroying the barracks. If they take control, they won't have anywhere to house their troops. The guns in the Queen's Bastion have been knocked out, and I'm afraid it won't be long until the Dauphin Bastion is silenced."

Thérèse returned with his meal, and he ate it quickly so he could get back to his post.

"*Merci beaucoup pour le repas*," he said, and then he was gone.

She had a lump in her throat when he left, and tears filled her eyes. It occurred to her that she missed his presence in their lives these past few weeks. She didn't know if she was feeling sorry for Marie-Louise or if she had a soft spot in her heart for him. Perhaps it was a little of both. She wondered if Marguerite and Madame Peré missed their husbands. If they did, they kept their thoughts to themselves. Gabriel's injury had not yet healed, and he continued to convalesce in the King's Hospital. Capitaine Peré remained a British prisoner of war and would probably not be reunited with his family until the end of the conflict. Don't be silly, she told herself. Of course, the women missed their husbands and worried about them when they were absent. The only person she should miss was her beloved husband, Nicolas, and no one else would ever take his place. It was then that she remembered the letter from him. She reached into her pocket and pulled it out. She broke the seal of wax with her finger, unfolded the pages and began to read.

January 20, 1757

My Dearest Thérèse,

It saddens me to think of you reading this letter from me, for it means that I am no longer by your side. I gave this letter to Père Aubré for safekeeping and asked him to give it to you in the event of my passing. I pray God to give you the strength to overcome my loss and any other atrocities in your life. Please know that I will be with you in spirit. I have taught you all that I know about the cod fishery, and I have faith that you will be able to fill the role of fishing proprietress in my absence. I have spoken with my dear friend and employee, André Belliveau, and he has offered to look out for you. So, do not be afraid to reach out to him if you are in need of his help.

I want you to know how much I love you and our little sons. I cherished the time I had with you and the children, even if it was short-lived. I know that you will be sad if something happens to me, but I pray that you are able to find happiness again. I pray that my family remains healthy, and that you are able to find peace during these tumultuous times. It is my wish for you to move on with your life and re-marry if the opportunity presents itself.

Give my love to Pierre and Philippe, and tell them that I will be looking over them.

Love,

Nicolas

She folded the letter and put it back in her pocket. Tears stung her eyes and she choked back a sob. Tears rolled down her face and she wiped them away with her handkerchief. His voice echoed in her head, as if he was right beside her. He was a wise man, and his words touched her, but could she find it in her heart to re-marry?

# *Chapter Twenty-Nine*

**Louisbourg, Île Royale, July 26, 1758**

Thérèse woke to a nudge in her side. "Are you awake?" Marguerite whispered.

"I am now. What is wrong? Is it not still too early to rise?"

"I do not know what time it is, but I have been awake for a long time."

The shutters at the windows were closed tight to protect the glass from shattering, making the house dark night and day. Thérèse longed to see the sun and let its rays warm her face. The darkness made her feel sleepy. She yawned, stretched and rubbed sleep out of her eyes.

"It is so quiet, and I have not heard the guns for a long time."

"*Oui,* the cannons are silent. The silence gives me an eerie feeling. I wonder what is happening?"

The baby fussed, and Thérèse picked her up. The other children still slept, so she crawled out of the shelter and settled in the armchair to nurse Angélique. It was a relief to not hear the guns, but what did it mean?

Madame Peré emerged from the shelter where she had been sleeping with her daughters. "I wonder why it is so quiet this morning?"

"Thérèse and I were wondering the same thing," Marguerite said.

"My daughters still sleep, but I have been awake for hours. I wonder what news we will receive today." She smoothed out her skirts and straightened her cap. "I am going for a walk."

"You are? What for? Do you not think it is too dangerous to be out alone?" Marguerite asked.

"A little bit of fresh air will do me good. Do not worry about me. I am a grown woman, and I can take care of myself."

"Would you care for some company?" Marguerite asked.

"*Oui*, I would enjoy your company."

The baby fell asleep in Thérèse's arms, and she put her down in the cradle. She sat back down in her chair and leaned her head back. She breathed a sigh of relief to have a break from the fighting. Was it over? Or had a truce been called for some reason? She was wondering these questions when Marie-Louise crawled onto her lap.

"I miss my *papa*. When will he ever come back?"

Thérèse gave her a hug. "I know you do, *ma petitte.* I pray this war will be over soon, and your *papa* will come for you."

The little girl looked up at her with eyes full of hope. "There is no noise outside. Does that mean it is over?"

"We can only hope and pray that it is over."

The door opened and Madame Peré and Marguerite came in.

"What news do you bring?" Thérèse asked.

"We came upon a group of townspeople in conversation with Financial Administrator Prévost. I am acquainted with one of the merchants in the crowd, so I asked him what news he could share with us."

Marguerite busied herself by putting logs in the fireplace. Thérèse knew she kept herself busy when she was upset about something. The news must not be good, she thought.

"The last of the French warships were attacked last night. British sailors got onboard the *Prudent,* and when they tried to move the vessel, it was hard aground. It caught on fire and was completely destroyed."

"Thérèse touched her cross. "Was anyone killed?"

"*Non*. Some French sailors were taken prisoner, while others were able to get away and swim to shore. The *Bienfaisant* was captured. British long-boats were attached to the vessel, and they moved it to the other side of the harbour." Madame Peré shook her head. "The merchant said there are no other French warships left to protect us from the waterfront. There are breaches in the walls, and it is possible for the British to have an all-out assault on the town."

Thérèse gasped. "These last few weeks have been bad enough, but if there is another attack, we would surely all be killed."

Marguerite stood up from her crouched position at the hearth and nodded in agreement. "It would be a terrible nightmare for the townspeople," she said. "I pray for God to be with us in our time of need."

"Governor Drucourt has decided that the time has come for the French colony to surrender. A white flag of truce was hoisted to let the British know that he is sending a note requesting to negotiate terms for a surrender. A note was sent back from the British line stating that they will accept a surrender, but with no conditions. The garrison would surrender as prisoners of war, and without the honours of war. It seems that the war council was appalled by this treatment, and a note was sent back to the enemy asking for terms. A note came back to the war council to say that the answer must be yes or no to a surrender. The French have said no to the agreement and are willing to have an all-out attack with the British."

"*Mon dieu*, I pray it is not so," Thérèse said.

Madame Peré could only nod in agreement.

Marguerite had a fire going and she hung the kettle over the flames. "Would you like a cup of coffee, Madame Peré?"

"*Oui*, that would be a treat. We have not had coffee for many days now."

"How about you, Thérèse? Does coffee sound good to you, too?"

"*Oui, s'il vous plait.*"

The women sat together and enjoyed the hot liquid they had been deprived of for many weeks. The children bustled about the house, anxious to go outdoors but Madame Peré forbade them going out. She felt that it might be too dangerous for them to be out without adult supervision. The children whined and complained, but the women were pre-occupied. All they could do was wait, worry, and wonder what their fate would be if the British had a full-scale attack on the town.

Lieutenant Duval visited the Peré home in the afternoon.

"Can I offer you wine or rum?" Madame Peré asked.

"*Non, merci*, Madame. I cannot stay for long."

"What news do you bring us?" Thérèse asked. They all stood around the lieutenant at the door, anxiously hoping it was good news.

Lieutenant Duval frowned. "The garrison has chosen to surrender." The women sighed with relief. The lieutenant continued. "Prévost urged the war council to surrender unconditionally, for the sake of the civilian population and further French colonization."

"So, there will be no more attacks by the British then?" Madame Peré asked.

"*Non*, Madame. The fighting is over."

"*Merci Dieu!* What a relief," Madame Peré said.

Thérèse grabbed her cross again. She silently gave thanks that her family had survived safely.

"The disappointing news..." he continued.

Thérèse felt a sinking feeling in the pit of her stomach.

"Is that the British are stipulating that the garrison will all become prisoners of war and will be sent to England. The civilian population will be deported to France as soon as ships are available to transport them. The Louisbourg garrison must give up their weapons and colours. Officers have been allowed to keep their swords."

Madame Peré had a sad look on her face. Marguerite had tears in her eyes. Thérèse had mixed feelings. She would like to see her family, but she dreaded the thought of an ocean voyage with three children.

"Madame Laserre, may I have a private word with you?" Lieutenant Duval asked.

She was startled. What did he want to speak privately to her for? Marguerite's eyebrows shot up and Madame Peré had a pensive look on her face.

"May we speak privately in your parlour, Madame Peré?"

"*Mais oui*, take all the time you need," she gestured toward the parlour door.

Thérèse followed the lieutenant into the adjoining room.

"I am sure you are wondering why I asked to speak to you in private."

"*Oui*, lieutenant."

"Now that the French have surrendered, the colony will be in the hands of the British by this time tomorrow."

"*Oui*," she nodded.

"I know you are a widow with children. You are vulnerable, and I am afraid you may fall into the hands of the enemy and forced into marriage. I want to protect you and your children from becoming British subjects. I know we have not had time for a proper courtship, but these are unusual circumstances. I am asking for your hand in marriage. I am able to provide for you and your family, and I will keep you all safe. We can be wed today.

She was speechless. What was she going to tell him? She did not want to marry him. She did not need protection. She had survived this long without Nicolas, and she was sure she could fend off a British soldier. She had fended off Jacques Bouchet. She felt herself getting warm and her face turning crimson.

"Today!" She exclaimed, "I think it is too hasty. We hardly know each other."

"*Oui*, Madame. But time is not on our side. We need to marry today. If we wait until tomorrow or later, the English may not allow us to be wed. We will be living under British rule until we are sent from the colony."

She turned away from him to compose her thoughts.

"Madame, please consider my offer."

How could she think of marrying him? André would take Marie-Louise away, and she would never see either of them again. She loved the little girl as if she were her own daughter. But what of André? He had been a loyal friend to Nicolas and had stuck by her side after his death. It struck her then. Her feelings for André were more than friendship. But would he propose marriage to her? She was not sure. All she knew for certain was that she could not marry the lieutenant. She turned to face him.

"Lieutenant Duval, thank you for your proposal, but my answer is no. I cannot marry you."

"But why? What is standing in your way, Madame?"

She bowed her head so she wouldn't meet his gaze. "I do not wish to discuss my reasons with you. I am touched by your concern for me and my family, but my answer to your proposal is no."

"Very well, Madame. If you have a change of heart, my proposal still stands."

"She nodded. She knew her decision would not change.

He turned, with slumped shoulders, and left the room.

# *Chapter Thirty*

**Louisbourg, Île Royale, July 26-27, 1758**

The Peré home took on the normal bustle it had before the endless bombardment of the town over the past seven weeks. The first chore was to air out the house. Shutters and windows were open to let in the fresh air. Floors and surfaces were swept and wiped clean of dust and debris. Buckets of water were carried from the well to fill tubs for laundry. Marguerite gathered vegetables from the garden to make soup. The aroma from the pot simmering over the hearth made mouths water, and they were all anxious to sit down to a hot meal instead of the cold rations they lived on for days. The household was fortunate to still have flour in the larder, and Thérèse set to work making bread.

She was worried about Marie-Louise. She whined and clung to her skirts. Thérèse tried to get her interested in helping to knead the dough for the bread, but the child shook her head. Oh yes, she had a stubborn streak, just like her own children. She wanted her *papa* and would not be content until he strolled through the door. But where was he? Why had he not come to see her by now? She hoped he had a good reason for not coming to see the child. As the hours passed, she became impatient, and even annoyed with him. Then her annoyance turned to worry. What if he had been wounded, or worse, killed by a bomb? She touched her beloved cross.

Marguerite was anxious to see Gabriel, and in the afternoon, Madame Peré gave her permission to visit him in the King's Hospital. Thérèse was pleased when she returned with her husband holding onto her arm. The surgeons had declared him well enough to return home. He walked with a limp, and he told them that he would probably have this injury for the rest of his life. He was glad to be out the hospital and was looking forward to a home-cooked meal.

Marguerite settled her husband in a comfortable chair in the kitchen, so he was close to her while she worked.

Thérèse gave the couple some time to be alone together and decided to walk to visit Nicolas' grave. The bombing had taken its toll on the graveyard. Headstones lay in ruins, and crosses were toppled over. Nicolas' cross was intact, but it was tilted at an angle. She smiled when she noticed that the fishing hook still hung from one of the boards.

"Oh Nicolas, I miss you. The boys miss you too. I wish you could meet your baby daughter. You would be pleased to know that Marguerite named her Angélique. I remember that you thought it was a beautiful name." Her eyes blurred with tears, and she wiped them away with her handkerchief. I know that you don't want me to be sad, but I can't help it," she sniffed. "I am determined to move on, but there will always be a special place in my heart for you. The children and I will be leaving Louisbourg and returning to France. I will not be able to visit your marker anymore, but I believe your spirit will be with me wherever I am. Goodbye Nicolas, until we meet again one day."

She had just reached Rue Talouse when she saw André walking up the street toward her.

"Where have you been?" she called out to him. "Your little daughter has been waiting for you all day."

"*Je suis désolé,* Thérèse. I had planned to come for a visit as soon as the bombing stopped this morning, but the militia were asked to help remove rubble away from the Dauphin Gate and I helped with the cleanup."

"Couldn't you have taken a few minutes to come and see your daughter?"

"I should have made the effort to visit her earlier in the day, but there is so much destruction to be cleaned up."

"She has been upset today, and I was at a loss to console her. Are you on your way to the Peré home now?"

"*Oui,* I am on my way there right now."

"*Très bien.* I am glad. I will walk with you."

"This siege has been so hard on the children and adults alike."

"*Oui*, it has been a tough time for all of us, and I worry about the days ahead of us. I do not look forward to an ocean voyage with small children."

He nodded. "I know, and I wonder what will become of us when we reach France?"

"*Oui*, the future is so uncertain for us all. I hope that I can find a way for me and my children to travel to La Rochelle, where my father and brother live."

"Before we reach the house, I'd like to take a few moments to talk to you."

"*Mais oui*, what is it you want to talk to me about?"

"Well, now that the colony will be in the hands of the British, colonists may not be allowed to marry by this time tomorrow."

She wondered if he was getting around to asking for her hand in marriage. If so, she knew in her heart what her answer would be.

"We are both widowed, and we both have children. Marie-Louise needs a *maman*, and I know she adores you. And your sons need a *papa*. They will need a male figure in their lives." He cleared his throat before continuing. "What I am asking is, will you marry me?"

She looked up into his eyes and said," *Oui*, André. I will be your wife."

"He smiled and kissed her on both cheeks. She smiled back at him. "And I would love to be a *maman* to Marie-Louise. She has become like one of my own children."

He put his arm through hers. "Let us go and give our families the good news, and then we will go to Père Aubré and have him marry us. It is my understanding that there are many marriages happening today, and he has offered to leave his door open all night for this reason."

She smiled, feeling at peace for the first time in months.

# *Author's Note*

Thérèse, her family and her friends are fictional characters, but the story is based on historical facts, prior to and during the Seven Years' War between Britain and France, from 1755 to 1763. Thérèse experienced events that women of that time period would have lived through. After the French surrendered the colony of Île Royale to Britain in 1758, the French colonists were deported to France aboard British transports, never to see Louisbourg again. The British Army destroyed the fortifications in 1760, so France could not reclaim the colony like they had done in 1748. One quarter of the fortified town was re-constructed in the 1960's, and it is a national historic site of Canada. It is a living history museum that depicts life in the eighteenth century.

# *About The Author*

Struthers is a counsellor, a traveller, and a storyteller. As a lover of historical fiction, she has visited historical sites and museums across Canada. She was inspired to write A Prayer for Thérèse after touring the Fortress of Louisbourg National Historic Site in Cape Breton, Nova Scotia. This visit spurred her deep dive into the realities of 18th-century colonial life and the challenges facing women in that period. In 2015, she deepened her understanding of the French colonies with a two-week immersive volunteering and research experience at the Fortress of Louisbourg National Historic Site, where she collaborated with staff to capture the details of life on Île Royale. A Prayer for Thérèse encapsulates the rich, sinuous history of Louisbourg through Elizabeth's nuanced characters and vibrant storytelling.

Elizabeth has a master's degree in social work and fifteen years' experience as a vocational counselor for adults with disabilities. She believes in providing equal opportunities for all persons, and this commitment informs her writing. She was trained by Sage Hill writing programs in 2016, and her short stories were recognized by the Lake Winnipeg Writing Group.

She now lives in Winnipeg with her cat, kitty Karmella.

Printed in Canada